ALIENS FOR DINNER

Welcome to Veggie World and Planet Rose! When a liking for Chinese food led her to fantasise about 'doorways' to other worlds, Lesley Howarth knew that *The Takeaway Tales* would be very bizarre or very strongly flavoured. In then end, they turned out to be both. '*The Tales* have tremendous pace,' Lesley says. 'I have to race to capture the characters, and the landscape feels like a real place. Whenever I go to my local takeaway, I think of the spot my characters landed in, in the middle of the floor, after their adventures. I can't resist staring at the microwave in case it bangs and sends us to Veggie World!'

Luckily Lesley Howarth is able to keep her feet on the ground long enough to relate these tales. Her novel *Maphead* won the Guardian Fiction Award for 1995 and her short story collections for Hodder include *Quirx 1: Welcome to Inner Space* and *Quirx 2: The Edge of the World*.

The
Takeaway
Tales

ALIENS
FOR DINNER

LESLEY
HOWARTH

Hodder
Children's
Books

a division of Hodder Headline plc

A Catalogue record for this book is available from
the British Library

ISBN 0 7472 73979 7

Typeset by Avon Dataset Ltd, Bidford-on-Avon, Warks

Printed and bound in Great Britain by
Clays Ltd, St Ives plc

Hodder Children's Books
A Division of Hodder Headline plc
338 Euston Road
London NW1 3BH

CONTENTS

1

MICROWAVING DAISY

Sinclair usually watered the yuccas before he went to school. His aunt Ping never watered them, so, in the end, he did. He couldn't bear to see the big, spear-leafed plants gasping in the window under the neon sign which said *China House Takeaway*, with nothing to drink but condensation from a hundred people's dinners. It was amazing how quickly they dried out. They needed a drink every day, which meant they drank eighty millilitres times seven, which would be about half a litre of water a *week*.

Sinclair liked working things out. His dad was fond of pointing out how clever Sinclair was. He could add up a meal for five with side-orders of Sweet & Sour, Soft Noodles, Chips and Mushrooms, in less time than it took to write it all down, which Sinclair never did. He never needed to. He could *see* it all in his mind, and a number just floated up. The number was always right. Millions of people had checked him, and no one knew how he did it, and he couldn't *explain* how he did it, because he didn't know himself.

He kept a calculator beside him, just for show.

Sometimes people would come in who saw quite a small boy taking and adding up orders and they didn't trust Sinclair's figures. Then he could stab the calculator to show them he was right. He didn't bother to look at it – he knew what the total would be.

The regulars never even looked at him. They wrote out a cheque straight away, or handed over their cash. They knew Sinclair was the sharpest thing in the China House Takeaway since Aunt Ping had dulled her cleaver on too many Peking Ducks. They never bothered to argue, whatever Sinclair said.

—Seven pounds, sixty-three. Sinclair would say, tearing off a numbered ticket. And the customer – Mr Davey, probably, Mr Davey was in every night – would sit down on a plastic chair with their ticket and quietly watch the telly or pick up *The Sun*. And the yuccas in the window would clack as the door breezed open and the bell rang and another customer lounged against Sinclair's counter and rolled the numbers on the menu on his or her tongue—

—Seventy-one – Shrimp Foo Young – what's that?

—Chinese omelette. Rice is extra, Sinclair would patiently recite.

—Hmm – has number sixty-eight got noodles in it?

—Beef Chow Mein. All Chow Mein dishes have noodles.

—Um, then I'll have fifty-one—

—Beef Chop Suey – with rice?

—And a pancake roll.

Sinclair would write down the orders and post

them through the plastic strip curtain to Aunt Ping in the kitchen. Sometimes he'd help Aunt Ping, if things got really busy, usually by microwaving rice in the battered old mike by the strip curtain. Sometimes he microwaved pancake rolls. Sometimes he microwaved pencils. One day, when he was really bored and the door hadn't dinged for a while and the telly droned and the fryers hissed quietly in the background, he thought he'd microwave Daisy.

Daisy was the only fish with a name in the tank of tropical fishes in the window. The only reason Daisy had a name, was that once she fell out on the floor and a customer scooped her up and slipped her back into her tank and said: *Oops-a-daisy.* The reason she fell – or jumped – out on the floor, was because of a new fish that Sinclair's dad had put into the tank the previous day, which followed Daisy around and harassed her.

The new fish died pretty soon after that, though, and Daisy never jumped again.

Instead, she swam round and round. How boring, Sinclair thought. Then he thought he'd mike her and see what happened. He didn't think too much about it. He just fished her out and did it.

She hadn't been revolving three seconds before something happened to Sinclair. The last thing he saw was Kevin Lee – Kevin Lee, sitting waiting for his chicken and prawn balls, with his stupid hair with SCUM bleached into it or something. Sinclair hated Kevin Lee . . .

and then the microwaves hit him on a strangely-charged wavelength, a wavelength which changed everything . . .

and he remembered Aunt Ping saying she'd change it—

that old oven leaked radiation—

radio waves, wasn't it, or something?

the door hadn't fitted properly for ages

she was sure it was dangerous these days—

BANG! went the microwave. Sinclair felt himself falling.

And then he was in a boat on a darkened sea . . .

Not asleep, not awake, maybe dreaming, Sinclair wondered what would happen as the other person – a woman – got out of the boat to wade over shimmering turquoise reefs, in darkness, to the shore.

—*See you later – hold the sail*, she said, or seemed to say.

Sinclair held the sail. The shore seemed a long way off. Under the water the fishes shimmered. The moon let him see his sail, the sea, the shore under a dull light – duller, when clouds passed over it. He held the sail as long as he could. Under the water there were sharks. Then he fell asleep.

He slept – woke – still in darkness, heard the clapping of the sails – approaching oars – and a gruff voice –

—Get in!

—What?

—Hurry, the sailor said. —We haven't much time.

Sinclair climbed into the sailor's boat, and

underneath him Fish World glimmered.

—Now row! the sailor said. —Row for your life!

—But why? Sinclair wanted to know.

They rowed as though the world would end.

At last they reached the shore—

On shore – *Run*! the sailor said, beaching his boat.
—Go – run! The world's ending!

Sinclair ran, he didn't know where.

He saw people who snapped into monsters with shining red and green skins and dinosaur-spikes down their backs – *people who weren't really people at all*, the sailor tried to warn him –

—*Run and hide! Run for your life!*

Sinclair swallowed and looked at the sea. Then he walked calmly into it, up to his neck and over it, deep into the turquoise shallows and sat down on the shimmering reefs. Over him the sky lit up in a tremendous flash that illuminated every anemone, every grouper and lion fish, every worm and pimple on every shell. Sinclair knew his world was gone.

This would be his world now.

BANG!

Back in the China House kitchen, a flash in the old microwave oven by the strip curtain sent Aunt Ping scurrying for Sinclair.

—Sinclair, what are you doing? *Are you miking pencils again*?

But Sinclair couldn't be found. In the end his cousin Mae took the orders, having slipped poor

Daisy back into her tank. No wonder Sinclair had legged it, Mae thought furiously. Microwaving a helpless creature. How could he *be* so cruel? Just *wait* till she caught up with him, then he'd know what helpless felt like, heartless little toad. Just because you were clever – and Sinclair was *very* clever – didn't mean you shouldn't have feelings, or *feel* for anything else. If Mae had her way, the world would be vegetarian, and everyone would be *all* feelings and no one would shred or stir-fry anything with eyes ever *again*.

But that was in her perfect world. Mae sighed. Her perfect Veggie World wasn't about to come true. Instead, the real world was filled with Sinclairs – perfectly clever but thoughtless folk, downing animals every day.

—Two Satay Mixed Vegetables, Aunt Ping rapped out – Come on, Mae, wake up.

Mae woke up. Still dreaming about her ideal Veggie World, where nothing microwaved anything else without asking its permission first, Mae Ling Peters put a dish of Thai mixed vegetables into the chatty old mike by the strip curtain and punched the hardly-working button that sometimes stayed in so you couldn't stop it, that said *Cook*. With a hum, the microwaves started and the vegetables revolved in a stately way on the turntable as radiation spilled out round the hardly-fitting door and bathed Mae – and everyone else in the China House that night – in strangely-warped rays . . .

The last thing Mae saw was Aunt Ping – Aunt Ping in her grease-splashed apron, shaking a fiery wok over the furnace-flame she called her cooker. Then the microwaves hit her – rays that were strangely changed, that had already strangely changed Sinclair . . .

Aunt Ping felt hot and bothered. Not only were they really busy that night, but that no-good old microwave was banging and flashing again and Sinclair had disappeared and Mae was so *slow*—

—Mae! she shouted. —Two Satay Mixed Veg! Sometimes I think I'm talking to myself – *Mae – hurry up – are you there*?

Suddenly Aunt Ping wasn't even there herself. Her wok had disappeared, even her apron. No longer was Mr Niles leaning heavily over the counter, his stomach, already bloated from too many chicken curries for it to matter very much if he ate one more, practically oozing over it. Aunt Ping's other regulars had disappeared, as well. Mr Davey, Saddo of the Decade, had lost his hangdog grin; David Selwyn, the regularest regular, had flashed away with a bang; even Kevin Lee, still awaiting his prawn balls, seemed to lift his head and flash away.

—*Well*. Feeling more than a little uneasy about her wok – somewhere her wok was overheating – Aunt Ping set her hands on her hips and examined her new surroundings. Whatever had happened, she would wake up soon from this very peculiar dream.

And so would Dim Sum the cat, who seemed to have dreamed it with her.

2

FISH WORLD

Sinclair opened his eyes. Around him the reef glimmered purple and orange and phosphorescent blue. Over it, fishes of every kind darted and eyed him up. He was safe for a while – but for how long? Grey reef sharks weren't far away. Panic, and they'd sense it through the water. They could probably smell him already. Sinclair tried to penetrate the night world of oceans around him. He needed a way to live – a way to be safe, and survive. Fish World was a dangerous place. He could be eaten at any time.

How would he, Species Takeaway Assistant, sub-species Sinclair Kuet, eat and not be eaten? What would his strategy be? Would he be a night-time current feeder, a top-of-the-food-chain predator, or would he graze off the reef? Would he hide to escape predators himself, or would he rely on speed? Which fishes posed no threat, and which were dangerous? What about the reef itself – weren't any likely hidey-holes going to be occupied already by octopus or slimy mandarin fish or other ambush experts?

Surprising himself by his knowledge of coral sea

fishes, Sinclair moved forward as though in a dream, and the reef slipped away underneath him. Breathing easily in some fish-like way he didn't even have to think about – breathing presented no problem, this was *his* world now – Sinclair drifted on with no effort at all. With no effort at all, he slipped over the edge of a cliff and out into unprotected water.

—Woh!

An unprotected moment was all it took. It was that easy to find yourself naked – or on something else's menu. Sinclair stopped, poised in mid-ocean. He was looking at the side of a mountain. Below him the reef fell away into nameless bottoms and impenetrable gloom. What creatures lived in those bottoms? What – why – did he feel he wasn't alone?

The grouper met his gaze imperturbably. It was a large, ugly, horny fish not particularly afraid of anything except very large octopuses and reef sharks.

—Ugly git, Sinclair told it.

The grouper bit a piece out of his sweater.

—Charming, Sinclair told it. —Don't mind *me*.

And he smacked the grouper over the head, but the water made his smack into a pat. The grouper came close, then closer. Sinclair even let it touch his ear. Then he brought down his arm and the grouper sped away, leaving a cloud of ground-up shell particles it had been eating some time before, for Sinclair to enjoy.

He thought he'd follow it anyway. A thick fish wouldn't entrap him, Sinclair felt sure. He had to be easy in Fish World, and a good start had to be using any fish that would let him for cover, food, or any slimy advantage in a world that was one gigantic fish dinner for someone – and Sinclair intended to choose the menu, no way was he going to be *on* it.

He followed the grouper effortlessly until it began to be frightened and sped ahead. Sinclair kept up with it easily, he didn't know how. At last they entered a narrow, dark place between corals. Overhanging fingers of tube coral clawed at Sinclair's clothes as he wriggled between them. The grouper slowed, flicking from side to side, so that it could eye Sinclair through distinctly unfriendly-looking pupils.

—I didn't mean to pat you, Sinclair told the grouper as it turned and deliberately rammed him. —You're not having another pat, no way.

The grouper gummed his jumper – it tried to gnaw on his shoulder – Sinclair pushed it away. The grouper had horny teeth. Big as a football – bigger – it had beige skin with blackish spots and a mouth the size of Wembley. It backed off and fanned its fins in the current. When it came in again, it came in like a torpedo, meaning, but narrowly missing, to take off a piece of his ear.

Sinclair felt his heart thump. He felt his chest would burst. What, was he going to be eaten already, by something as stupid as *this*?

He tucked himself into a crevice, feeling the coral scrape his skin. When the grouper came in again, it followed a thin thread of blood. Sinclair looked at his leg. Great. Now every shark that wasn't eating already would smell the next course on the menu – number 77 – lightly-grazed Sinclair with Noodles, or Sinclair Chow Mein. If he didn't want to be sharkfood, he'd better do something quick. Suddenly flooded with determination to rid himself quickly of the ugly and persistent grouper, Sinclair turned to face it.

What did animals do under threat? Usually they made themselves bigger. Puffing his cheeks out and thrusting out his chest and his belly, Sinclair extended his arms and legs. Then he crossed his eyes and blew loads of bubbles. Blurggg! Rurrgle-blur! Bleahglghgh!

It worked. With a flick of its meaty tail the grouper turned, leaving a cloud of shell-particle farts behind it. As it crossed in front of him Sinclair whacked it one, but it only felt like punching a football. When the shell particle cloud had cleared, the grouper had gone.

Sinclair allowed himself to sink. He could do this pretty easily by exhaling. If he wanted to rise, he inhaled – water, oxygen-in-water, whatever. His gills seemed to deal with it, anyway. He even had a lateral line. Lifting his shirt, he saw what looked like pinholes crossing his skin. The feel of the water across them told him loads of things – water pressure, disturbances many miles off, which way up he was. Right now they told him something big was approaching.

The tarpon hung in mid-ocean, making its presence felt. It was a big fish – more than two metres in length – and actually weighed sixty-eight kilograms. Along

11

one side of its mouth it bore the scars of a struggle with a sports fisherman who *had* thought he'd haul up the tarpon to gasp its life out on his deck for nothing much more than the thrill of having his picture taken beside it; but after a half-hour tussle and the loss of an expensive line, had thought he might not bother, after all. The tarpon had carried the sportsman's hook in its jaw for some time after that, which accounted for its lop-sided grimace. Dark blue on top, silver beneath, it was an impressive fish for all that, mainly because of its size and intensely miserable expression.

But Sinclair could hardly look at it straight without laughing. What was it *like*? Did its face say Mr Davey, or *what*? Mr Davey taught R.E. in Sinclair's school, and always looked as though he himself *personally* were crossing the Red Sea with the Israelites when he tried to make himself heard above everyone who didn't want to listen to him, no matter what he had to say – probably why he always looked miserable. If Mr Davey had had to announce that everyone had won a millon on the Lottery, he probably would have had trouble making himself heard. I don't know why he bothers, Sinclair had told his dad. No one ever listens to him, plus he's miserable-looking. 'Lugubrious', you mean, Sinclair's dad, who was big on cryptic crosswords, had said. Sinclair looked up 'lugubrious' and found that it meant gloomy.

Exactly like the wardrobe-sized tarpon that regarded him steadily from a distance of less than two metres. Sinclair assessed the threat along both sides of his body via his tingling lateral line. A big tarpon. Avoids the hook of a hunter. Eats prey quite a bit smaller than itself – how much smaller?

—*I'm a harmless reef-grazer, right?* Sinclair spread his arms. —*You don't want to eat me. I'm too much trouble. I'd stick in your throat or something.*

The tarpon turned on its stately way.—You're not on my menu, its eyes seemed to say. Yellow and black – grisly taste, or what?

Sinclair considered his sweater and jeans. The grouper hadn't minded his yellow sweater. Probably it had thought it was a kind of a shell, with pink flesh somewhere inside it. The tarpon wasn't much brighter than the grouper. But the tarpon, at least, saw it for what it was – yellow sweater, black jeans – the code that said *I taste grim and am possibly poisonous – come and have a go, if you think you're hard enough.*

He could work out a way to live, after all. He had some simple defences. If he kept a low profile, tarpons would tolerate his presence, and groupers he could handle. Sharks would always be a problem, of course – but grazing the reef would protect him. He only had to find something he could actually stand to *eat*, and—

A shadow crossing Fish World dimmed its gorgeous corals. Sinclair the Fish looked up. Above him spotted dolphins zipped and plunged through the sunlit surface water, shadowing some largish creature – like a whale-shark or a ray or something, or – Sinclair's whole body tingled – could it be? —*a boat.*

Effortlessly Sinclair rose through the water and

13

found he could match the dolphins for speed, mainly because the boat – it *was* a boat – wasn't travelling much faster than two dipping oars could make it. Joyfully exploding upwards in a shower of spray, Sinclair glimpsed a girl rowing, sunlight glancing off her oars, before he crashed back into the water. Next time he rose more carefully. He might actually be scary, he realised.

But actually, *she* was more scary. It didn't seem to matter that he'd risen, fully-formed, from the ocean with no visible means of support and no place to rise up *from*. All that seemed to matter was that he got in the boat really quickly.

She assessed him coolly as he clung to the side.
—Get in.
—Really?
—Quick.
—What's this place called? Sinclair asked, being able to see now that he was in a boat, that of course his reef circled an atoll – in fact, *was* an atoll. Coral had to grow on something, and here it had grown on itself, over and over and over – finally making a doughnut-shape that had poked up out of the water and clothed itself in palms. The atoll was classic desert-island stuff, complete with white beaches washed by a green lagoon. Gorgeous. Tiny. Probably really remote.
—So where are we? Sinclair repeated.
—Bikini, the girl in the boat said, sorting out her oars.
—Yeah? Sinclair frowned. He'd asked her where

14

they were, not what she was *wearing*.

—They sunk radioactive ships around here. Used for target vessels.

—Yeah? Sinclair said, again.

—This is Bikini Reef, the girl said.—Site of nuclear testing in the sixties?

Sinclair swallowed. —Nuclear testing?

—Mushroom clouds, you know, multo radiation – everything poisoned for hundreds of miles for hundreds of years, you know? Where have you *been*? the girl said.

—In Fish World, Sinclair told her.

The girl in the boat looked at him.

—You'll have to help me row. We've got two thousand miles to go before we hit Hawaii.

—I don't want to hit Hawaii. I work in our shop – the China House Takeaway – and I'd like to go back there now, please.

—Take this, the girl in the boat said, handing him one of her oars. —My name's Alma. Now *row*.

Sinclair took an oar and worked out in his head pretty instantly how many million times he'd have to dip it and pull, dip it and pull, to reach two thousand miles to Hawaii. It wasn't a pretty figure. Not one he'd put in his top ten of figures you'd live to reach.

Beneath him Fish World glimmered. Sinclair bent to his oar. He had fishes on the brain – it had made him dream he was one of them – had brought him to a boat in the ocean, after something weird had happened – something he might have caused. That flash overhead – when he just arrived – had had something to do with it.

Now he had to row two thousand miles. It was his own fault, he supposed. It would never have happened, he had to admit, if he hadn't microwaved Daisy.

3

Veggie World

Waking up in Veggie World where nothing hurt anything else, and Exhibition Cows wandered fearlessly across busy roads in front of commuter buses, Mae Ling Peters had one thought, and one thought only – *Sinclair – you beast – where are you?*

It didn't occur to her to ask what *year* it was. But she very soon found out via the MediaMax screen over the bus rank.

The giant screen pulsed with glowing headlines:

NEWS UPDATE MAY 6TH 2032*NEWS UPDATE MAY 6TH 2032* NEWS UPDATE MAY **IYAMA STORM PACIFIC*FISHERMEN CAUGHT UNAWARES*IYAMA STORM** PACIFIC*FISHERMEN CAUGHT UNAWARES* IYAMA STORM PACIFIC*FISHERMEN CAUGHT

Boatloads of refugees fleeing Iyama agression are being attacked by pirate vessels posing as fellow—
—Kevin Lee – what are you doing in *that*?
Mae Ling gaped. The boy she'd addressed turned.

He eyed her up and down.

—In what? he asked her coldly.

—Those clothes. Mae Ling covered her mouth.
—Black and orange, I mean – *yuk*.

—Standard Balment Line colours, Kevin Lee
returned coldly, the bleached lettering in his hair
saying SHED instead of SCUM like it usually did.

—My name's Redmond, not Kevin Lee, in case
you want to know.

—You what?

—Bus monkeys wear Line colours, okay? I don't
get to choose what I wear.

—Line colours?

—Here's my ride. Got to go.

Mae Ling watched, astounded, as Kevin/Redmond
swung easily onto a huge triple-decker bus – like a
bus she'd never seen in her *life* before – which matched
his uniform, swirl for swirl, in extravagant whorls of
black and orange. BALMENT LINE the electronic
announcement strip circling the bus announced
endlessly. KINGSLEY – JACKSON ISLAND – THE
BRONX – ALL STOPS EAST OF QUEENS ★
BALMENT LINE ♥ TIDY COMMUTERS
WELCOME TO BUSLINK – KINGSLEY –
JACKSON ISLAND – THE BRONX – ALL STOPS
EAST OF QUEENS –

—You're right, Mae yelled, —You match your bus,
you multicolour nerd, Kevin Lee!

But Kevin/Redmond didn't hear her. He nodded
and waved as the giant Balment Line bus pulled out,

and it seemed to Mae Ling Peters that so far from still waiting on his prawn balls back in the China House Takeaway, Kevin Lee didn't *know* he was Kevin Lee any more – but that didn't make him any less the madman she knew he was.

Mae Ling watched the enormous luxury three-tier buses on the Bus Rank jostle for position after Kevin Lee had pulled out. Different bus lines had different colours – and uniformed boys to match. She numbered the Lines on her fingers:

Black and orange – Balment Line.

Green and gold – Holden Line.

Blue and white – Corinthian.

Maroon and white – Town & Country.

Red and gold – Imperial.

The buses were ready to go. But not a single one could pull out, Mae Ling noticed, until a lowing line of cattle had swung across the bus rank one by one, their horns tipped with some flashing metal, their udders wrinkled and empty, their really quite ordinary black-and-white coats looking, for all the world, like another kind of bus-boys' livery.

—Take their time, don't they? Mae Ling found herself saying to a woman in a Holden Line queue.

The woman snorted. —They will.

—Where's the farmer? Mae Ling wanted to know. —Why aren't they in a field?

—Farmer? The woman looked puzzled. —They're Exhibition Cows.

—That makes them special?

—Special?

—What about cows in fields?

—*All* cows are Exhibition Cows.

There was a lot she didn't know, Mae Ling realised. A lot she'd have to learn. She turned back to MediaMax news:

NEWS UPDATE MAY 6TH 2032 ★ NEWS UPDATE 6TH MAY 2032 ★ NEWS UPDATE 6TH **RADIATION PUZZLES BOFFINS★RADIA-TION PUZZLES BOFFINS★RADIATION PUZZLES BOFFINS★RADIATION PUZZLES** *An unexplained burst of radiation on the site of former nuclear test ground Bikini Atoll has left scientists mystified. A small boat was sighted in the area, and there is some uncertainty about damage to plants and animals—*

Mae Ling swallowed angrily. *A small boat sighted in the area – some uncertainty about damage to plants and animals –* What kind of Future World was it, that allowed things like *that* to happen? What had happened to her? What had happened to the China House? What had she done, when the microwave flashed? Whatever had happened since – *had it got to do with Satay Mixed Vegetables?*

Feeling kind of peckish, and feeling some odd-shaped cards in her pocket – one of them looked like a credit card and said *Netlink Masterpass* – Mae Ling went to the takeaway on New Street, which wasn't new at all and had actually been constructed in 2017, *some nineteen years in the future.*

—Whaddya want? the girl at the counter asked.

—Something vegetarian.

—Veg-a-*whad*-ian?

—No meat – you know?

—Meat?

—Dead animal flesh?

It was as if she'd mentioned dead *human* flesh. The girl behind the counter wrinkled her nose.

—We got this, this, this or this. She indicated the photos above her.

Mae Ling scanned the photos of lurid and unfamiliar food over the counter. The Future World takeaway had a nice line in Soya SurfBurgers, but what was battered Iyama, when it was at home? Or Ritalin Extra Coke?

—I only just got here, Mae Ling confided. —I suppose I know *when* – but can you tell me *where* I am?

—You got the Blue Schooner Takeaway on New Street.

—Yes, but what place, I mean?

—How come you mean, what place?

—I mean, said Mae Ling patiently, I-don't-know-where-I-am-so-please-can-you-tell-me?

—How about that. The girl behind the counter appealed to her customers incredulously. —She's in the Animal City and she don't know where she is. She don't even know her order—

—I'll take battered Iyama, Mae Ling said firmly, —

just so long as it's got no meat in it.

—With chili-chips or potato subs?

—Potato subs, please, Mae Ling said, without a clue what they were. —You haven't seen a boy come in – about ten – glasses, short hair?

The girl behind the counter wasn't more than ten, herself. Ripping off a numbered ticket, she handed it to Mae. —I see 'em all the time, she said, nodding towards the bus rank opposite. —Mr Parker over there, he snatches boys every day.

—He snatches boys?

—For bus monkeys – dresses 'em in uniform, SHED's 'em up so they work for him for next to nothing – but what's it to me, you know?

—SHED's 'em up? May Ling repeated.

—SHED – makes you stupid, you know? You don't even want to *go* there. Blue cheese dressing okay?

—Please.

Feeling her head spin with new information with slightly sinister overtones, Mae Ling Peters watched the Blue Schooner Takeaway assistant with the badge saying 'Alberta James' scoop potato substitute fries on to a sizzling battered Iyama steak. She didn't even know what it was. She didn't want battered Iyama. She didn't want blue cheese dressing. She didn't even want to *be* there.

All she wanted was plain old Aunt Ping shouting orders, Dim Sum the cat in the window, Sinclair the beast answering the phone – in the fiery, whistling kitchen of the China House Takeaway in the world –

the real, the only, world – she'd somehow left behind.

She could her Aunt Ping now . . .

—*Chicken Chow Mein! Two Egg Fried Rice!*

The tish-tish sound of something being moved about in very hot oil filled the China House waiting room. Behind Mae Ling's head her Uncle Wei and Cousin Sang criss-crossed the kitchen with hot woks. 'Neighbours' blared out on the telly.

—*Yes, please? Sinclair answered the phone. At the same time, he took down an order.* —*Eight-eighty, please.*

A blast of cold air came in at the door as another customer blew in.

—*Bye-bye. Sinclair put down the phone and passed in an order. Immediately the phone rang again.* —*Hello, China House Takeaway?*

The customer he'd just handed a ticket to sat down with the Mirror *and a tired expression, glancing at 'Neighbours' over the heads of the other people waiting. On the wall to Mae Ling's left a split-bamboo calendar announced: Year of the Rat 1996 – issued by B.J. Brothers Frozen Food. No one had even noticed it was two years out of date.*

—*Number twenny-five – than' you. Uncle Wei handed out the latest order in a Sunny Frites cardboard box. The yucca plants in the window in their square, 'oriental-style' clay pots nodded and clacked in the wind of the door as it opened and closed and another customer went out into the night hugging hot food to his chest.*

The big telly, the gas heater, the enormous menu on the wall with Specials outlined in red, the hiss and sizzle of hot fat, the shish of veg in the wok, the hum of the fume extractor

23

– it all spelt the unique fug and dazzle of the China House Takeaway to Mae Ling – and to Sinclair. She could still remember him as a baby, squishing noodles between his fat fingers. Sinclair had sat under the counter and watched it all going on over his head since he very first could remember – about eight years ago – which made him about as old as the nodding yuccas in the window.

And Mae Ling about as old as the yuccas plus Dim Sum the cat . . .

Mae Ling stirred. *Forget about Sinclair – and going home – until you can suss things out.* Taking her unwelcome Iyama steak, she found a cool place in Central Park. Central Park had changed a lot since *she'd* ever seen it in movies. Cows wandered freely over the paths and flicked their tails in fly-filled wallows under trees. Pigs rooted everywhere under rubbish bins. Sheep and really quite fat lambs lay asleep where people stepped over them.

Sinclair was somewhere in this world, she knew. Hadn't the microwave banged and flashed just a second before she'd used it, when Sinclair had disappeared? *An unexplained burst of radiation has left scientists mystified* . . . the greasy old microwave in the China House kitchen had something to do with it, all right.

Mae Ling sniffed her Iyama. Finally she took a bite. Whatever it was, she hoped and prayed it was vegetable in origin. Wasn't this Veggie World?

4

IYAMA!

—Microwaves are short, high-frequency radio waves lying roughly between infra red waves and conventional radio waves, Sinclair recited. —See Electromagnetic radiation; Radio. Microwaves have many applications in radio and television, radar, meteorology, satellite communications—

—Uh – oh. Company. Alma drew in her oar.

Sinclair followed Alma's gaze, saw nothing more remarkable than a junk bearing down on them quickly, and returned to his run-down on microwaves. If he stopped reciting the Encarta entry now, he'd have to go back to the beginning and start all over again. Sinclair liked memorising things. He memorised anything from chemical and mathematical formulae to recipes, car manuals, the contents list of his mother's foundation and Herbal Astringent Cleanser, bus time-tables, random bits of Encarta and Internet addresses and the Drilling and Boring sections of Yellow Pages. He could even recite the entire season's basketball fixtures for Tarmouth Pirates plus scores for every game. But once he got started on one of his lists, he *had* to go on to the end. Sinclair was funny like that.

—distance measuring, and research into the properties of matter. Microwave ovens operate by—

—See that junk? Alma pointed. —Let's hope they're not Iyama.

—agitating the water molecules in food, causing them to vibrate, which produces heat.

—Shut up and get down in the boat.

—Wha—?

—Lie down in the boat. Alma pulled him down, glancing fearfully after the junk, fast catching up with them now. —What are you, stupid? —just *do* it.

Sinclair finished the rest of his microwaves recital through his teeth in the bottom of the boat.

—Exposure to microwaves is dangerous mainly when high densities of microwave radiation are involved, as with masars. Maser, acronym for Microwave Amplification by Stimulated Emission of Radiation. May cause burns, cataracts, damage to nervous system. The possible dangers of long-term exposure to low-level microwaves are not yet known, but—

—You don't say a *word* if they board us, right?

—exposure levels are limited, in general, to ten milliwatts per square centimetre.

—You let me do the talking—

—Stricter limits are placed on microwave ovens, Sinclair mumbled, apologetically.

—Did you hear what I said?

—Microwaves, Microsoft Encarta. Able to look up

now he'd finished, Sinclair considered the junk.

Closing on them rapidly, with every surge and swell bringing it closer yet and raising them up into view – like sitting ducks, Alma said – the junk's sails stood taut in the wind that brought them the smell of it, now – a smell like leather and spice with a hint of metal. The smell was very unusual, Sinclair thought; like eating cinnamon toast in a welder's mask, if you could, which Sinclair doubted. A junk in mid-Pacific, weird or what – shouldn't it be somewhere like China?

—Poo – Iyama! Smell 'em? Alma shivered and wrinkled her nose.

Sinclair nodded. It was the strangest smell in the world. Now he could hear the junk's rust-coloured lugsails straining and clapping in the wind. The blunt-nosed prow rushed down on them bearing its name – *Annaho* – before it, impetuous, unfriendly, as though it would never stop. At last it stood over them, taller, by far, than he'd imagined – and *still* the junk came on.

Sinclair gasped. —Why don't they stop?

—They will.

—They're going to ram us!

—No, they won't – they've seen us now, worse luck.

At the last minute the junk turned, its sails suddenly slackening as its long rudder swept it out of the wind. It drifted majestically alongside, riding the waves like a dragon about to spring. Sinclair peeped out of the boat. The junk's high poop deck had what looked like living quarters in it. Somebody must be steering it. Where was everybody?

The boat bobbed; the junk dipped; the slack sails flapped their battens.

Still there was no one in sight.

And then suddenly, there was.

—Hello, smiler. The man on deck looked down out of a blazing sky. He wore a batik scarf, polynesian style, wound tightly around his head. —Mind if we come aboard?

Alma rose unsteadily. —We haven't got any food.

—Let me be the judge of that.

Sinclair watched as the man swung himself aboard – and another, and another man after him; all dressed in dirty sailcloth with cummerbunds of scarlet and cowrie shells at their necks. They looked, he thought, like pirates. One of them looked like David Selwyn. One of them *was* David Selwyn. Sinclair felt his pulse race. David Selwyn, *who ate Chinese practically every night*. He flushed and started to stammer. It happened sometimes that he couldn't stop, when he got over-excited.

—D – David, David Selwyn, I saw you come in the other night when you had Sweet and Sour, remember, and Uncle Wei put in rice instead of chips, and you said, I always have chips and *I* said—

—Where have you come from? The first sailcloth pirate checked Sinclair with a stern-looking hand. — The Marshall Group, perhaps?

—The Marshall Group – what was it, a band?

28

Unable to take his eyes off David Selwyn, Sinclair's heart hammered. Alma answered for them.

—There's been an accident. We're lost off a ship.

—What ship would that be?

—It went down.

—Nevertheless. The pirate waited.

Sinclair looked from the pirate to Alma. He didn't like the air of menace underlying his tone very much.

Alma made an effort. —The ship was the *Dayton Ohio*. She went down beyond Bikini. It was horrible. A storm hit us. I think we got struck by lightning.

The pirate nodded. His eyes swept the boat.

—There has been a kind of anomaly.

—An anomaly?

—An *event*. He put a peculiar emphasis on the word and looked at Alma.

—What was it?

—You tell me. His eyes seemed to bore into Alma. Then they bored into Sinclair

Sinclair felt a tic coming on. He really felt very distressed.

The third pirate took his hand. —Come on, he said, —come on with me. You look as though you need a drink.

—Can I have a milk-shake? asked Sinclair.

—You come on with me, you can have anything you want. The third pirate, who was long and gangling with laughing eyes under his gay polynesian scarf, helped Sinclair out of the boat, up the ladder, over the rail and on to the junk. —What will it be, he said, — coconut ice, or rum baba?

—It's all right. Sinclair looked down on Alma. — It's all right, really. Come on.

A shadow crossed Alma's face. As she followed Sinclair up the rope ladder on to the mysterious-looking junk riding the darkening waves over Fish World, already the first pirate was lashing their boat to the stern, *along with two or three other boats*, Alma noticed, her heart sinking suddenly inside her.

Sinclair didn't know the worst. He didn't know anything at all. In the hands of their enemies, all at sea, the third pirate with the laughing eyes was the nearest thing to a friend they had in the world. He looked all right. He smelled all right. The other two were definitely Iyama. The pirate with the kindly face and manner looked as though he were human, all right.

But even he could be one of them.

5

THE HISTORY CHANNEL

—Hello, Smiler – got yourself some grub?

—I'll deck it, if it says that one more time, Alma whispered through gritted teeth.

—Him, you mean – not *it*, Sinclair whispered back.

—Can we have some orange juice? Alma put on a smile.

The crewman's cowries clicked together on his neck as he bent to fill a glass with orange liquid. He offered it to Alma.

—Cheers.

Alma tasted it and grimaced.

—Pretty *near* orange juice – but not quite.

The crewman frowned. —Not?

—Of course, not all orange juice tastes as good as this, Alma said, diplomatically.

The crewman waited until Alma set down her glass of not-really-orange-juice; then made to fill it up, but Alma covered the glass with her hand and shook her head impatiently.

—Had enough, shipmate, hey?

He smiled. His name was Rameth. Napes was the

other crewman, who looked like – *was* – David Selwyn. Then there was Robert Ames – Robert Ames, of the kindly eyes, who'd gone back up on deck earlier. Sinclair wished he hadn't. He liked the cut of his jib. That was what Robert Ames had said to him earlier.

—Sit here, young feller, you're a likely lad. I like the cut of your jib.

Sinclair didn't like the cut of Napes' jib much. Napes had treated him with enormous disdain since Sinclair had greeted him as David.

Sinclair had tried to put it right. —You look like a friend of mine, I mean, really *really* like him – d'you like Chinese food? David Selwyn does. David Selwyn comes in the takeaway six nights out of seven – all right, five of seven. Know what he likes best? Aunt Ping puts the fryers on right away – chicken curry with chips and a pancake roll, usually it's seven pounds eighty-three unless he has extra rice, then it's eight twenty-three – and anyway, you look just like him.

Napes was unimpressed. He served them a meal of strange-looking fruits quite politely. Rameth looked in now and again. But Sinclair couldn't help noticing that the hatch to the deck remained closed. He looked around the cabin. We must be making a few knots, he thought. Judging by the clang of the pots.

It was easy for Sinclair to memorise a list of the things that he saw:

Barrels of beer – it had to be – labelled 'Old Bones

Tipsy Peculiar'; a chronometer; desk; compasses; maps; cans of navy beans; jars labelled 'Salt Cake' and 'Acid', another labelled 'Weevils'; a fourth labelled 'Isinglass'; a galley filled to bursting with the remains of many meals, none of them yet cleared away. Hanging from the beams, pots and pans and fish-hooks; from the bunks, fish-nets and needles. In every available space a clutter of plastic roping, floats and clothing and socks and plimsolls and coffee-cups welded to tables with salt-grease and ancient biscuits stuck to maps told a tale of untidy confusion. Vats labelled 'Proteins' and 'Growth Medium' made Sinclair feel slightly uncomfortable.

There were other things, too – things Sinclair didn't associate with a bunch of untidy sailors. The clump of human-looking hair bunched around a nail by a port-hole didn't appeal to him much. He supposed it was someone's wig. Also he didn't like the teeth that swam in a glass of pinkish liquid amongst a muddle of bottled squid. Of course, they were someone's false teeth. But a pulse in Sinclair's neck told him they weren't. He looked away before he really could see the bits of flesh around them that trailed away in the bottom of the glass. He fuzzed his eyes over the galley, as well. What *were* those things stuck to the plates?

On the opposite side of the room, under a groaning bulkhead and partly set into it, a wide but very thin-screen TV smeared with fish-blood – he supposed – caught Sinclair's attention. Sinclair got up; examined

PROTEINS

SALT
CAKE

Acid

Weavils

BEANS
NAV.

GROWTH
MEDIUM

Old Bones
Tipsy
Peculiar

it; pressed its only available button. He licked his finger as a newsreader flickered on-screen. It was a pretty distressed-looking set. MEDIAMAX Multi Task Transmission Unit said its interestingly salty frame. Sinclair returned to his fruit, a furry affair that tasted like pear-drops inside. Fruit was all very well – but wasn't there anything else?

Suddenly really hungry, —No burgers here, then? he enquired.

—Burgers? Alma widened her eyes. —I don't see any, do you?

—Don't you *have* burgers here? Sinclair felt quite cross. —Like, ground-up meat in a roll?

—No one eats ground-up anything. That would mean killing an animal.

—No meat at *all* – no way. Sinclair's turn to widen his eyes.

—Sssh – Alma said. —Turn it up.

—What?

—The Max – just wave – that's it.

Sinclair was nearest the MediaMax. He waved his arm and the picture came up, as Alma had said it would.

*NEWS UPDATE MAY 6TH 2032*NEWS UP S*UPDATE MAY 6TH 2032*NEWS UPDATE*
Fishing has been resumed in the Marshall Islands, despite caesium levels in sand. Environmental experts say that fishing should be discouraged—

2032? They had to be kidding – what did it *mean*, May 6th, 2032? Sinclair flapped his hand; the Max flicked through several channels. A brash-looking ad filled the screen showing shiny young people in uniforms:

Don't miss our Special Offer Dinner – Buy any Laver Burger and get a Cheese Topper Iyama Steak Meal for less than the price of your coffee!! Blue Schooner Comfort Stations – where Iyama steaks cost less. Don't miss our Special Offer

—I don't understand. Sinclair put down his strange-looking fruit. —What *are* Iyamas? he said.

—Iyam*a*.

—Whatever.

—You want to know about Iyama? Alma paged the History Channel by making a gesture Sinclair couldn't quite follow. —There you go, Mr Kuet. The History Channel. Press 1.

Sinclair searched the MediaMax for a way to press any '1'. At last he saw it – a touch panel way up onscreen. You didn't have to be near it. you simply crooked a finger. Immediately a reptile flashed up. The strangest reptile, Sinclair thought, he'd ever seen in his life – *yet it looked familiar.* Where had he seen it – in dreams?

—*One of the first sightings*, the commentary told him over a picture of the strange-looking reptile crouching under the shadow of a wall, *one of the first sightings occurred in Tapaulo, Mexico. It all started in '89, when a reptile-like alien caught running around the town surprised Mrs Rameres on her balcony—*

—Is *that* an Iyama? Sinclair wanted to know.

Alma nodded. —What did you think – they're *pretty*?

—*It had greenish skin*, Mrs Rameres reported from her balcony. —*It surprised me right here – it looked kind of angry, kind of frightened. It had blueish-red spines down its back – it made a run at me, and jumped right over the railings here and landed right there in the garden.* She pointed into her garden. —*I don't know what happened to it after, but my neighbour said the soldiers caught it and took it away in a van. It had webbed feet. I saw it. They were hanging out of the tarpaulin.*

Sinclair shuddered. —Scary, he said.

—You don't know the scary part yet. Alma made an impatient gesture, and the MediaMax hurried on:

—*spines are distinctive, also a metallic smell. A tendency to snap back into human form has led to a policy of Identi-Chip Confirmation for any police or government appointment, to block Iyama infiltration—*

—What does it mean? Sinclair frowned. —I don't understand, he said.

—You heard, Alma told him. —'*A tendency to snap back into human form.*' What, d'you want it spelled out?

—Please. Sinclair nodded humbly.

—They look like people, right? But suddenly they can change.

Onscreen a perfectly ordinary-looking man behind a bank teller's counter suddenly burst out of his clothes.

—It's like the Incredible Hulk, Sinclair said, happily.

But it wasn't like the Incredible Hulk at all. It was more like the end of the world, as the people onscreen screamed and fought and fell over each other to get away from the strangely-changed teller. Suddenly greenish, the teller rose. His blue-red spines, caught on the bank's security cameras, were clearly visible erupting out of the back of his suit. With sudden and horrible agility, the Iyama leapt over the counter and into the midst of the screaming people. With a strangely lurching motion, on plainly webbed feet, it legged it out of the bank, the bits of its suit streaming after it.

—It's *horrible*, Sinclair said.

—It's overplayed, this Iyama business. Entering silently behind them, Rameth snapped off the Max with a hiss. —There aren't as many as you think.

—They say they can look like people. Alma watched Rameth coolly.

—How can a thing like *that* look like a person?

—That's what I'd like to know.

Rameth's mouth, decidedly green-tinged now, twitched almost imperceptibly. It seemed to be deciding something. Finally it tried to smile.

—Chin up, Smiler, it said to Sinclair, trying to ruffle his hair.

Sinclair ducked away.

—I want to go home, he said.

—Why, that's just we're headed, shipmate.

Sinclair brightened. —Really?

—See if what I say isn't right. Rameth opened the

38

hatch and the sunlight flooded in.—Go up and ask the charmer.

6

THE CHARMER

—Rameth says we're going home, right? The thing is – Sinclair squatted on deck beside the lean man with the charming smile – sorry, I sat on your belt—

—Cummerbund, if you please. Robert Ames rescued the end of his sash, clearly proud of its sheen. —A cummerbund is no ordinary belt. Especially one such as this. The colour of blood, sir, he added.

Sinclair looked at him uncertainly.

—Whatever. The thing is, it's weird here, and I live in a takeaway, in probably another world not this one, so how can I go home?

—Homeward bound, eh? Robert Ames took his pipe out of his mouth. —Grips your heart, don't it – like the last fire of a sunset or that first glimpse of a low island in the morning, with the wind set fair and a whisper of landfall in the air, or a salty tear– he looked at Sinclair – on a picture of your mother, far from home, when you figure yourself crossing the old street, approaching the old front door; opening it; seeing a figure; crying: *Mother! I'm home!*

Sinclair pictured the scene. To his surprise, a hot

tear ran down his face and plopped on his sleeve. *Mum*, he thought, *I'm OK. I hope you're OK, too*. He looked at Robert Ames with new respect. He seemed like a magician or something, to charm a tear from his eye when he never knew he had any.

Alma seated herself gingerly a little way away from them. She didn't trust this man, if he was a man, nor anyone else, on this junk.

—What was that?

A clicking sound of spines.

—That? said Robert Ames. —Why, the birds flying overhead.

—It wasn't – it was something on deck – there it is again.

—It's nothing but the wind in the rigging.

—If you say so.

—Take a tip from Bob Ames—

—I might.

Robert Ames considered Alma, his head half-cocked, with a humorous look, on one side.

—A'n't you the jumpy one, though?

Alma wasn't laughing. She sniffed the wind; no metal smell, at least – not from Robert Ames, anyway. She braced herself as the junk raced on, dipping and bowing, sails clapping, spray fizzing on the cargo-laden deck. What *were* they carrying, anyhow?

—Look! Alma pointed. —Spotted dolphins!

—They're luring females away, Sinclair said. —Separating them out, so they can fight over them later.

—How do you know? Alma looked at him.

—I don't know how I know. Sinclair tried to look humble. —Except, I was once a fish.

—How many were with you? The charmer addressed himself to Alma. His kindly eyes invited her to confide in him. But Alma put up her screens.

—I'm sorry?

—On the *Dayton Ohio*.

—I don't want to talk about it.

Terrible memories raced through Alma's mind. Sinclair watched her curiously as tears streamed down her face. He had no idea why she was crying, but he knew that people who were crying usually liked you to hug them, so he gave it his best shot, and sure enough, Alma leaned on him just as though he were comforting her, which, in a way, he was.

—You've got a good friend there, Robert Ames said, his kindly brown eyes taking them in.

Alma nodded weakly. Everything seemed too much.

—Friends are like gold in the dross of life, Robert Ames went on. —Little flecks in the stream, and we must pan for them as we can, and keep them while we may.

—Excuse me? Sinclair looked blank.

—A man found a jewel, you know. But he didn't know what it was – he thought it was a stone, and he gave it away. Years later, he read in the paper that that stone had polished and sold, and his heart ached that he had had it, and didn't know. But did that make it valuable?

—It was just a stone to him.

—And to others, a blazing jewel.

—I like the things you say, Sinclair said, —but I don't understand what they mean.

Robert Ames laughed.

—They call me the Teller of Tales, he said. —And they gave me this ring in the Islands.

He showed them a silver ring set with a turquoise T.

—T for Tales, Sinclair said happily, who'd have killed for a ring like that.

—Or Teller. Robert Ames smiled.

He patted the deck beside him.

—Come – sit here, he said.

Alma still wasn't sure. Did he know he was with Iyama on this vessel? He must know – how could he not?

—You do know you're with Iyama? I mean – you must know that.

Robert Ames flushed. —Oh, he said, —I don't think so.

—Oh, *yes* so – Alma said, —are you *blind* or something?

Robert Ames knocked out his pipe and put on a grave expression. She'd given her position away quite seriously, Alma realised, in bringing up Iyama and pushing them into his face.

—Then again, she said, —I might be paranoid.

Robert Ames closed his eyes. —I *did* hear a tale of a ship overturned by an iceberg—

—The *Titanic*, Sinclair said.

—No, it was the *Dayton Ohio*—

—It wasn't an iceberg, it was a – Alma clammed up suddenly, remembering not to speak of the wreck of the *Dayton Ohio*. No use throwing accusations about. ActionPeace had to be careful.

—and all who sailed in her perished, Robert Ames continued softly – *isn't that so?*

Something in his eyes warned her to agree with him.

—That's right, Alma nodded. —Everyone – except us.

Already a sickly-metallic odour reached her nostrils and she realised – of course – that their whole conversation was being overheard by the Iyama Rameth, whose spines, spines she'd heard raised earlier, were visible now behind the cargo blocks. Her heart pounded. *You do know you're with Iyama – are you blind, or something?* What else had she said? What else had she given away?

Robert Ames continued smoothly:—No point in looking for survivors, now. I expect you were the last to get out?

—The very last, said Alma. —Whose are those boats tied aft?

—The boats tied aft are visitors – but not from the *Dayton*, you know.

—And this boat is?

—The *Annaho*. We happened to be in the area—

—Fishing? Alma watched him.

—Fishing, exactly right – and we would, of course,

44

have been glad to help; but unfortunately there were no survivors but you, and – what did you say your name was?

—Sinclair, said Sinclair.

—What does it mean?

Sinclair looked blank. What did *any* name mean? Then he thought of something.

—It means, he said, —Calculator-of-Sums.

The Teller of Tales bent his head. —Very good, he said.

—I've got Asperger's, Sinclair volunteered, unusually.

—Asperger's what?

—Syndrome. It's very mild, Sinclair assured Robert Ames. —It means I don't know about some things, but I know a lot about others.

—What things do you know about?

—I know the basketball league results, home games and away, this season *and* the last. I know about vectors and quadratic equations. But I don't know why people cry, plus I microwaved Daisy. Mae Ling says I don't have feelings. But I get in tempers sometimes.

The Teller of Tales looked at him.

—I think there's four kinds of people, don't you? Sinclair was gabbling, now. —Hunky and nice, hunky and not nice, not hunky and nice, not hunky and not nice—

—Which am I? Robert Ames interrupted.

Sinclair took a long look at him. —Not hunky and nice, he decided.

The Teller of Tales threw back his head and laughed.

—You're a strange one, he said.

Alma hardly heard them. Those boats – she didn't know what she'd hoped. Being netted by Iyama was better than dying at sea in an open boat, *but only just*. And it wasn't over yet. It was just beginning.

A very slight scraping sound drew Alma's attention; then the very absurd sight of a line of reddish-blue spines creeping away behind the pale blue-green tarpaulins covering the cargo, whatever it was, announced that Rameth had heard enough. Iyama weren't too clever – what did it think, she couldn't *see* it?

At last she saw it – Rameth – checking their course on the poop deck. She wasn't the only one to notice.

—He's gone now. You're safe. Robert Ames looked at Alma.

Alma looked back at him levelly. —*It's* gone, you mean.

—Did you hear the tale of the boy who cried wolf—

They weren't going to hear it now. Rameth, the poop-deck watch, windmilled its arms and threw back its head and uttered the strangest sound.

*EE*YOAR-OH! EEEYOAR-*OH!*

Sinclair looked up. —What was that?

—The look-out's sighted something – it's a war-cry, Alma said.

Robert Ames paled and got up. —Better keep your heads down. There could be trouble ahead.

7

THE GRIP

Trouble, Sinclair thought, in the shape of an enemy junk. Borne on a blustering wind by indigo-blue and purple sails of a different size and cut to their own, it didn't take a genius to see that the barbaric-looking junk – Sinclair could smell it now – would all-too-soon catch up with them. Its crow's nest crowded with Iyama flying banners of saffron and gold, the junk, which was rather larger than *Annaho* all round, seemed to be making more sail and more ground with every passing moment.

—Where should we go? Sinclair pulled on Robert Ames' sleeve. —What should we do – *hide*?

But the blood had gone to Robert Ames' head. Already his eyes were wild with a kind of excitement. With a quick movement he shook out a telescope and applied his eye like a hawk.

—As I thought – the *Ulan Bator*. We're in for it, now, all right.

—But what should we *do*? Sinclair insisted.

—It's the grip, lad – fight or fall. They've the advantage of us in everything but manoeuvrability, but do what you can, when you can, there's a trim feller – it's every man for himself.

Girding himself with his blood-red sash, Robert Ames plunged away.

Still the overbearing junk came on; Sinclair could make out the spars now, dense with armed Iyama, dipping and rising closer with every surging sea. A pulse beat fast in his head. For some reason the *Toxic Crusaders* theme went round and round in his brain.

—Why do they want to fight us? he asked, as the sinister-looking *Ulan Bator* grew larger and more distinct with every second. He could hear its war-drum now, beating out time to the rowers.

—That's what Iyama do. Plus there's food aboard.

Sinclair had never seen hands wrung before, but Alma was actually wringing hers.

—They all have Masers – nowhere's safe—

—What *are* Masers, anyway?

Alma looked around her, then hissed:—You *know* what Masers are—

—I do?

—You told me. In the boat.

Sinclair recalled his list. —M.A.S.E.R., acronym for Microwave Amplification by Stimulated Emission of Radiation. May cause burns, cataracts, damage to nervous system. —He actually knew a bit more. —Paramagnetic masers use energy transitions corresponding to the orientations of the magnetic moments of paramegnetic ions in crystalline substances placed in an external magnetic field. Different

49

frequencies can be obtained by varying the magnetic field, thus allowing—

—*Please shut up.* Alma held her head. —Don't you understand? We're about to be fried – *there's no place we can go.*

—Get near something magnetic. Sinclair scouted around. —It'll alter the frequencies, probably.

In the end they settled under the ship's compass in a rickety shack on the poop-deck. The helm swung unattended as Rameth and company – more Iyama crewmen than could ever have been suspected – swarmed on the deck below. Sinclair took the helm and swung the junk into the wind. They would get a great view of the battle. The spot was a pretty exposed one. But Sinclair was sure it was right.

Robert Ames appeared beside them. —There's nothing like war, sir – nothing.

He licked his lips and slung from his shoulders a strange-looking weapon on a heavily-embroidered strap, which although he'd never seen one before, Sinclair knew to be a Maser. He envied Robert Ames it's fancy handle and gorgeous carving, although what it was made of, he couldn't begin to guess. The amplified microwaves, Sinclair knew, were generated in the barrel – a longish electron tube, or magnetron, which gave it the look of a rifle. The built-in resonator controlling the frequency had been set to Max, Sinclair noted.

—A.1., said Robert Ames, squinting down his Maser barrel as enemy fire lanced in, shredding the rust-coloured lugsails and leaving them sheets of flame. His finger flickered; wavered; then something cut the air beside Sinclair Kuet's ear that left him blind and deafened to anything else. In a dream he saw a mast explode on the junk now set to ram him. But the *Ulan Bator* didn't falter. It would ram them any second.

—Hard-a-port! Robert Ames turned the helm decisively for Sinclair, hand over his hand, long be-ringed fingers over his. —Bring her alongside – that's it.

The burning boat nuzzled her enemy; then Robert Ames was gone. From the poop-deck of the junk *Annaho*, Sinclair Kuet and Alma Brand watched as the battle began; a battle they would never forget in their wildest dreams of conquest in deepest jungles, or their wildest fears of falling or flying or dying.

All in a dream the junk came on; in a dream Sinclair read *Ulan Bator* on her prow; and in a dream she rammed them. In a nightmare, horribly agile hordes of red-backed Iyama swarmed on board, just as nightmarishly countered by white lines of sailcloth-clothed *Annahos*, their spines bursting out of their sailcloth shirts as the battle lines wavered and clashed. With horrible ferocity a webbed foot clawed through their window; Alma smashed it away with anything she could find, sobbing as she fought it. Sinclair steadied the vessel against the wind. With the sails of both junks burning fiercely it was as much as he could do to keep the *Annaho* free of her enemy's falling spars and curiously-tongued ramming irons.

What more could he do? Indistinctly he made out the tall, lean figure of Robert Ames slashing down sail with a cutlass. Good man. Sinclair twitched and controlled himself. This was no time for tics. This was a time for action.

Individual scenes below imprinted themselves on his mind; he couldn't have told anyone how long the battle lasted; time stretched; was crowded; yet was still and long-lasting, forever, as amid that battle tumult a single Iyama turned to eye the poop-deck and raise its arm.

A Maser flashed in the sun.

—*Get down*! Alma screamed.

With a thud the parcel of amplified microwaves hit them, pushing a wave of air before it that burst in a dragon's-breath of flame. Sinclair felt the jolt through his nervous system, the flash lighting the back of his eyes, and electrifying his brain. Panting, he looked for Alma.

—What is it? she cried. —*Is it gone?*

The Maser-bolt had cut through the cabin entirely – through the haft of the helm – through the door, through the thickly-boarded deck, and into the hold below, leaving them singed and half-blinded. Sinclair staggered back, his jeans somehow stiff and crackling and welded onto his legs, noting with amazement Alma's Maser-shocked face with its orange-tinted skin and shock of frazzled hair, watching *him* in amazement, too. He wondered if he looked the same, or worse, as she did.

—Look! Alma pointed. —Down there!

Along the still-smoking line cut by the Maser a mess of writhing arms and hands was emerging up through the deck, clutching hand-holds of cargo tarpaulin, pulling it down and feeling for something – anything – on which to gain a hold.

—Prisoners! Alma said with horror. —Prisoners in the hold!

The struggle worsened as they watched, the desperate anemone of hands clutching men's legs as they fought, pulling down ropes and bill-hooks, boots and even a monkey, which screamed as it disappeared.

They would never get out that way, Sinclair could see. Poor old prisoners'd probably go down with the ship, if he couldn't avoid those grappling-irons thrown out by the *Ulan Bator* – the enemy ship – and how was he going to avoid them, with no helm left to steer by?

Seizing a rope, Sinclair wound it as fast as he could round and round the helm and through the shattered wheel. Bracing himself, he pulled to starboard as hard as ever he was able.

—Pull! he shouted. —*Help me!*

Alma strained behind him. It was going to be touch and go; if they cleared those hooks and irons, grappling now across the flaming, oil-licked water between the listing *Annaho* and the bullying *Ulan Bator*, still they might go down; unless the tide of the battle washed over to starboard, the port rails would kiss the sea and they would sink under the weight of

53

interlocked men and Iyama, and – all of them – go down fighting.

—*Harder*! Sinclair strained.

—We're sinking! Alma screamed over the battle. — *Can't you all move over?*

Slowly the *Annaho* was coming about – Sinclair could feel it – but would it be fast enough? What about those poor lost souls in the hold? If the *Annaho* sank, their poor white arms would wave out of sea-filled decks and fishes would thread their way through them, and they would never grasp anything again. Sinclair redoubled his efforts. No way would he let them all drown. But even Sinclair couldn't turn a junk without a wind to fill her sails.

Alma threw back her head. —A wind – please! She closed her eyes with fierce concentration. —*Please let a wind spring up*!

And suddenly the ends of Alma's hair lifted; the sails cracked full; an electric thrill passed through Sinclair's arms and into the helm, the ship; he lifted his head as the horizon, the sea, the sky, were lit by a tremendous flash. It seemed as though a bomb dropped, or a god had come down from his heaven. When Sinclair could see again, the decks were silent except for the spraying seas, and an unearthly light beamed down from a familiar face in the sky, except that it wasn't in the sky, the unearthly face *was* the sky, and—

—Aunt Ping! Sinclair gasped. —How is *she* here?

Sinclair held his breath as the sky stooped down and spoke:

—Help me! it drummed, through strange-sounding echoes. —Where am I? Help me – Sinclair – *are you there*?

8

BETRAYAL

Aunt Ping's giant face in the sky strained against an invisible film as though trapped in a polythene bag. A giant hand tried to break through – to reach out – to find him. He couldn't be sure she saw him, but Aunt Ping's eyes, each as large as an ocean, appealed for Sinclair to come.

—I'm coming! he cried, —Wait for me! Where are you – don't go – *Aunt Ping*!

But the face in the sky had gone. With a roar, the battle resumed; but now the tide had turned. Cowed by gods in the sky, seemingly with a message for the helmsman, the Iyama hordes of the *Ulan Bator* fought a desperate retreat. Cutting their sails free, they streamed away as if by magic; ignoring the cries of its wounded, the *Ulan Bator* disengaged and limped away, a still-smoking ruin of a junk.

At last Robert Ames stood alone on the poop, the *Annaho* Iyamas snapping back into men one by one on the rails below him and cheering, as Alma and Sinclair tried, but couldn't manage, to share their triumph.

—This is our chance to escape. Alma looked around for a hiding place. —They'll never know where we are now.

—What? Sinclair, still flushed from the battle, couldn't grasp what she meant.

—They aren't our friends. They're *dangerous*. Alma spelled it out for him. —It won't be long before they're looking for us – see?

Alma pointed. Sinclair looked. On the rails below them a reptile-like greenback twitched; clicked; and changed – *snap*! —retracting its red-blue spines into its back and its tail between its legs and its green-toned skin into 'human' skin and its reptile head into *Napes*, in what seemed the blink of an eye. With quick, reptilian moves of its head Napes searched the deck keenly, looking more than ever the image of David Selwyn, he of the constant ding at the door, the *man*, they called him, who ate his way most weekday nights through Special Chow Mein with Spare Ribs or Beef Curry plus Extra Noodles.

Napes/David Selwyn smelled the air, then swung in Sinclair's direction. Sinclair ducked, his heart pounding. It was weird to be hunted down by something which looked like a customer, but he mustn't be fooled by the David Selwyn-ness of it. Had he forgotten what they were? Watching Iyama snap into men and knowing what they *were* underneath took the edge off a sea-battle, somehow, reminding Sinclair sharply that he was half-guest, half-prisoner of alien thingummyniggles he didn't understand who were quite prepared to spear and throttle and barbecue *other* whatever-they-weres exactly like themselves and cheer about it afterwards. For one thing, he didn't want Napes to find him. For another, he was seriously scared. Alma was right about one thing. Mortal danger was what they were in, which was worse on a scale of a million than any other kind.

—Under the tarps – quick! Ducking under a tarpaulin between cargo-blocks held down by chains, Alma held up the edge for him to follow.

Sinclair hesitated. Just as he ducked in to join her, he thought he saw Robert Ames turn slowly in his direction.

—*Robert Ames looked at me*, Sinclair whispered, finally finding Alma in the smelly dark alleys between cargo bales.

—Think he saw us?

—Probably. What should we do – move?

—Too late – we'll have to trust him. Alma shook her head. —Come on, get further in.

Once deep in the darkness under the tarpaulins, between reeking wooden cases of something-or-other franked with mysterious signs, Sinclair sat down and waited for whatever would come next.

—You always know what to do, he told Alma admiringly.

He cocked his head to try to discern her face.

—What does *your* name mean?

—My name means *spirit*, Alma said. —What *is* this cargo, anyway?

Whatever it was, it smelled pretty foul. Alma wrinkled her nose.

—Smells like toast, Sinclair said.

—*Burnt* toast.

—Or plastic.

—What *was* that, that happened? Alma's voice took on an edgy tone. —That flash – and the face in the sky? And why did it say your name?

—I think it was my Aunt Ping arriving, only I think she's gone somewhere funny, funnier than this, I mean—

—Your Aunt *Ping* arriving?

—The microwave in the kitchen's gone weird, Sinclair admitted. —Uncle Wei meant to fix it, but Dad says it's knackered, just throw it away, only no-one went out and got a new one because Aunt Ping wants one more powerful, and Dad says it doesn't *matter*, what make we get but my Aunt thinks it does, so we go on using the old one, and sometimes it bangs and explodes, and it banged and sent me here when I put Daisy in it. Daisy's a fish, and I—

—*Sssh*. Alma clapped a hand over his mouth.

—Ahoy, shipmate! Napes was really near. —How much sail can we put on?

—How much sail have we left?

Robert Ames. Through a brass-ringed hole in his tarpaulin Sinclair could see him on deck, clearly now in command.

—You stay here, I'm moving, Alma whispered.

—Don't—

But before Sinclair could stop her, Alma had wriggled away.

Sinclair turned back to his spy-hole. He found himself trying to spot slits in the back of Robert Ames's shirt, despite feeling almost ashamed of himself, remembering Robert Ames lively brown eyes and his quizzical, half-humorous way of giving you all his attention and making you feel that nothing else mattered in the world, so long as you spoke together. Was it possible he was Iyama with eyes like that? Had spines sprouted out of Robert Ames's back in the heat of battle when he, Sinclair, hadn't seen him – as they had out of Napes' back – and Rameth's?

Sinclair was wary by now. He'd seen too much already – too many scenes in battle, too many small betrayals, sudden stabs and lunges, arms hacked and trodden on, bellies grappled with irons. He would never forget what he'd seen. Beside Robert Ames the body of the Iyama Rameth was only recognisable by the strips of clothing it had worn in the shape of a man, its half-hacked-off tail bleeding glutinous-looking brown blood over the rusty, burned sail it was wrapped in with half-a-dozen other mangled, half-human Iyama. *They did it to themselves*, Sinclair thought. *What horrible things they really are.*

Meanwhile, there was Robert Ames, casually coiling rope and overseeing the clean-up after the battle. Robert Ames, who may or may not be human and who may, or may not, keep their secret. Robert Ames, with their lives in his hands. Robert Ames, who knew where they were.

Napes watched Robert Ames as though the thought had flashed across and reached it.

—Seen them striplings, have you? it asked.

—They went overboard in the scrimmage—

—Saw 'em go overboard, did you? Napes watched Robert Ames.

—What, don't you believe me? Robert Ames said, lightly. He nodded at three waiting crewmen, who rapidly baling the bodies overboard in their sail, were quick to stand to attention.

Robert Ames looked coolly at Napes. Sinclair held his breath.

—I should think they're in Davey Jones locker, by now. Unless they're on the *Ulan Bator* – or stowed away in the biscuit.

—Don't joke with me, shipmate, where are they? Napes cast around for them. The deck stretched away between blocks of lashed-down cargo, empty except for ropes. —Won't I catch it, if they're gone.

—I'm acting captain now. Robert Ames brought out his pipe. —And I say they've gone overboard.

—And I say they haven't.

—Who do you report to?

—I've got secret orders, me. Napes' face darkened. Its back made a series of clicks. —Cross me at your peril, mate, know what I'm saying?

Robert Ames struck a match. His face glowed with flesh tones as he puffed and lit his pipe. At last he looked up with a changed face – how changed, it was hard to say.

—They're there, he said coolly, pointing them out with his pipe. —In the cargo. The boy's under the canvas. The girl's slipped aft in the boats.

Sinclair's ears burned. His face flamed with shame for Robert Ames. *Thanks a lot, mate. Anyday. Do the same for you.* He drew in his arms and legs as a burst of light flooded his hiding-place.

—Come out then, fishee-fishee – Napes fished for Sinclair with a boat hook and finally snagged him out. Sinclair wriggled and thrashed about – like the tarpon, he'd fight if he had to.

—Quiet down, now, fishee, Napes threatened, not unkindly. Not unkindly it tucked the struggling Sinclair under its arm and caught up the hatch with its foot – a webbed foot, Sinclair noticed – and thrust its fishee-fishee into the hold.

The hatch door slammed. Napes locked it. Then it turned for Alma.

9

THE HOLD

So – why were Iyama so interested in the survivors of the wreck of the *Dayton Ohio*, and what had happened to it? And why had Robert Ames insisted Alma agree with him that beside herself, there *were* no survivors – and all for the benefit of Rameth, now dead, whom Robert Ames had thought, had *known*, was hiding nearby to spy on them? And if he'd seemed in some way to be helping them then, *why had he just betrayed them?*

These and many other questions pulsed in Sinclair's brain as he picked himself up at the bottom of a rough wooden ladder, the light from the hatch, so recently slammed above him, dancing over his clothes as he felt his way through the darkness, or not-quite-darkness. Above him saw-blades bit through the deck as carpenters laboured to board up the smoking slit in the boards scorched by the Masers in battle.

Hee-haw, hee-haw, hee-haw – the ends of rough carpentry saws appeared and disappeared, taking off odd ends of planking. *Biff! Baff! Bang!* Rough planks were nailed on any-old-how, edges of webbed Iyama foot sometimes protruding through the deck as the carpenters, working hard, couldn't be bothered being human and let their feet hang down, sometimes so close you could grab them and *pull* – but what would be the point?

Through the daylight flashing in odd shapes as the hole closed gradually over him, Sinclair made out huddled shapes in the hold – people, lots of them, watching, as he watched, the saw-blades above them robbing them of light and a life-line. These were the prisoners who'd reached through that smoking slit in the deck so hungrily, clutching legs, feet, ropes, knives – even a screaming monkey, in a desperate bid to escape, their hands like so many octopus arms or the arms of some pink anemone. Now he, Sinclair, was a prisoner, too – and somewhere, so was Alma, thrust in after him after a fight and sobbing somewhere in the dark. Sinclair blinked. In a moment his eyes would get used to the murk, and then he would see where he was.

—Alma? he tried. —You there?

—Sinclair?

—Alma? said a third voice. —Alma – is that you?

—Boney – Mayo – *Mum*!

Alma's voice reached him through the darkness of the hold – where was she, who was she greeting? Sinclair stumbled; recovered himself. Spots of colour swam in front of his eyes, joining at last to form a picture. It was obvious, now, whose company he'd ended up in. In the hold – they had to be – were the survivors of the *Dayton Ohio*, the wreck Alma Brand had survived; why else would she call someone *Mum*?

—Sinclair – Mum. Alma introduced him. Alma was very happy. Sinclair was glad she was happy. He hoped she'd be happy every day of her life and that nothing bad would ever happen to her. He liked her as much as he'd ever liked anyone in the whole of the rest of his life, and that included his friend Miranda who was way more Asperger's than he was and only ever said *No* and *Mine* and the dates of future Wednesdays, and had terrible tempers, but was okay when you got to know her.

How long could a hug go on? Trying to understand it – how she felt, how the hug felt, how her mother felt – in the way he might try to understand a problem posed by the opposing angles in a triangle, Sinclair watched in a very odd light as Alma hugged her mother.

At last it seemed they could speak.

—Mind your head, said her mum.

Sinclair dodged as a saw came flashing around his ears; a shaft of light, filled with sawdust motes, made a halo around his head.

—Wo-h. He grinned. —Thank you.

—Where were you? I thought I might never *see* you again. I didn't know where your boat had gone. After the second flash, I mean – I woke up and then – I thought – I thought you'd – Alma hugged her mother again. At last she looked around her. —But this is bad – where we are.

—It's bad, all right. The friend she called Boney nodded.

—But they haven't got all of us yet, the friend she called Mayo added.

—There's no reason why they should. A tallish man rose beside Sinclair. —Unless, of course, someone tells them who's missing.

—So you *are* from the *Dayton Ohio*?

The tall man lifted his head and the light fell full on his face. —What do *you* think? he said.

Sinclair the Fish swallowed. His lateral lines tingled. He didn't think he could stand to meet the miserable-looking tarpon again, only this time *posing as a man* – a man named Mr Davey, R.E. teacher at school, last seen in the queue at the China House Takeaway wanting Special Dinner for One. Why did he keep meeting Daveys? Wasn't it enough he'd been seen as a fish? What next, Davey the horse or the chair? What about the other way round – would Daisy the fish pop up to remind him he'd stuck her in the microwave? *How would she look if she did*?

—Anything could happen to us now. Mr Davey smiled down on Sinclair, reminding him of a hundred grindingly boring afternoons in school. —But we're safe as long as the anomaly holds their attention.

—The anomaly?

—The explosion – the flash of radiation.

—What about Robert Ames? Alma demanded. — Is he Iyama, or what?

Mr Davey's face clouded. —I haven't been able to

decide. That man's a mystery, somehow—

—That *man* – you think?

—It's not often I can't tell Iyama straight off, but you can't be sure with Bob Ames.

—I think he is, Alma said.

—I think he isn't, said Sinclair.—But why did he tell David Selwyn—

—Napes.

—Why did he dob us in to Napes?

—There's only one reason.

—He might just be keeping in with them.

Alma laughed hollowly. —Right.

Mayo opened a foil pack. 'Sta-Fresh' said the wrapper.

Boney groaned. —What have you got there – Iyama steak?

—Better than nothing, isn't it? Mayo unwrapped the sea-sodden sandwich and offered some to Alma. —I've been saving something for you, in case – you know – you turned up.

Alma squeezed her hand.

—I thought you said you were veggie, Sinclair said.

Alma took a bite. —I am.

—I thought this was Veggie World, where no-one eats ground-up anything.

Alma looked at him with her mouth full.

—So how come you're eating Iyamas? Sinclair persisted. How could she *want* to eat them?

—They're not animals.

—They're not plants. How can you call yourself

68

veggie and still eat Iyama sandwich?

—Iyama aren't anything to *do* with this planet—

—So?

—they come from somewhere else.

—And that lets us kill them?

—You kill pigs and dogs.

—I'm sorry?

—You, in the past – I know what you are. You're not off a ship or anything—

—I never said I was—

—you're one of *those*.

—Excuse me – one of *those*?

—People caught in doors. Like Second World War pilots lost off Bermuda in mists, that kind of thing. You've been there since – Alma narrowed her eyes – since about '96, I'd say.

— '98, actually, you're way off line. And just because it's the past we don't kill dogs, all right?

—Just pigs and cows and sheep.

—Whatever.

—Whatever, yourself.

Sinclair felt sad. He'd thought Alma Brand was his friend. Now she knew he was out of the past – he *supposed* he was out of the past – she seemed to think everyone in 1998 was a howling caveman or something, just because they ate sheep and pigs and kept chickens in very small cages. She said he'd been caught in a door or lost in a mist. He kind of wished he had. This future world was *a* future world, not *the* future world, he hoped. Here people ate Iyama steak sandwich, probably with web-feet for garnish, which made them no better than Iyama themselves, and they couldn't even see it. Sinclair pictured shark's fin soup, something his Uncle Wei made very occasionally, as a family treat not a takeaway – what about Iyama soup, he wondered, what would *that* have in it, a reddish-blue spine in the middle? Mae Ling would be horrified . . .

—There are many doors to my father's house, Mr Davey had tried to comfort him. Sinclair had backed off. —Yeah, right.

What was he talking about? No one liked Mr Davey much. Some people even called him Able, some kind of stupid nick-name, Sinclair didn't know why. No one spoke in front of him. No one laughed at his jokes, which was pretty easy actually, since all of them were pathetic, a bit like the giant tarpon's expression, which Sinclair couldn't forget.

Sinclair felt left out. But he wasn't the only outsider. Two or three times the others in the hold had been talking and shut up abruptly when Mr Davey got up. The discussion, whatever it was, would be turned off suddenly, like a tap. It even rubbed off on Sinclair. Even Alma turned away from him, when she saw Mr Davey sleep beside him, even though he tried to explain he never *wanted* him to. Alma seemed cold towards him. Even Sinclair knew cold when he felt it.

—Friends? he whispered.

—Friends. Alma said. But he didn't know whether she meant it.

Friends or not, they had problems. Days passed in which nothing came down through the hatch but bits of fish Sinclair recognised. He felt as though he were eating his friends – he *was* eating his friends. But at least he found out a few things. Like no-one ate fish but him and Mr Davey, because everyone else was veggie and held out for fruit, which came down now and again in a bucket with 'orange juice' and something that tasted like porridge, but had a much slimier texture.

—This *food*. Sinclair grimaced.

—They make it in vats in the galley.

—What – they *make* fruit and orange juice?

Mayo nodded. —It isn't real. That's why it tastes so foul.

It didn't matter much. As the seas grew more boisterous beneath them, no one could eat very much. Every single person was sea-sick, including Sinclair, who was spectacularly sick in his shoes – everyone except Mr Davey. Then the next day Mr Davey was sick, and the atmosphere changed completely.

Suddenly everyone included them. It was as if the sun had come out.

—Where are we *going*? Sinclair groaned, holding his stomach.

—San Francisco, I expect, Alma answered brightly, helping poor Mr Davey out of his soiled jacket and buzzing it into a bucket.

Everyone had something to say. They even joked about hurling, after Sinclair showed them his shoes.

He'd scoured them out with a rag, which turned out to be a boy named Everard's shirt, drying out on a beam after *he'd* hurled all over Mayo.

In the midst of this warm, friendly feeling, Sinclair felt deeply confused. He and Mr Davey had been cold-shouldered for days, it was hard to tell how many, since one day was much like another. Now Mr Davey was sick in his pockets, and suddenly everything was sunshine. After the evening bucket of porridge and fins and something that looked like mangoes but tasted like tyres, he found out why.

—You thought he was an Iyama *spy*?

—Could've been, said Mayo. —They can look like anyone they want.

—You mean – it might not be *him*?

—It might not be *you*, Mayo said. —He isn't with us, anyway.

—He isn't? So where did he come from?

—How do I know? He turned up just before you did.

—But why would he be a spy?

Mayo shrugged. —He wasn't sick. Can't trust anyone, can you?

It turned out *Iyama were never sick*, so the moment Mr Davey threw up his guts he was human, and in the clear, and so was Sinclair.

—You could've told me, Sinclair grumbled. —No one tells me anything.

—That's 'cos you're a time-warp weirdo, Alma told him.

—Even time-warp weirdos need to know what's going on. Sinclair paused, then jumped in. —So what happened to the *Dayton Ohio*?

A pause in everyone's movements meant that everyone had heard his question; Alma's mother stopped washing pants out in sea-water; Mayo stopped writing a sea-sodden diary; the men at the end of the hold looked up over the pinches of tobacco they were splitting and dividing between them; even boy Everard rolled on to his elbow and significantly lifted his head. The tallow lantern swung in the roof, lighting eyes and the angles of faces – faces now turned towards Sinclair. At least, Sinclair thought, they'll talk, now that Mr Davey's been sick.

—There was a flash – two flashes – Alma looked upset already. —We went down in under two minutes—

—In ninety seconds, actually. The *Dayton Ohio* is – was – a marine research vessel. It turned out Boney – Captain Bonaventure – was the one who would talk most of all. —We're measuring caesium levels in fish. Iyama don't want us to.

—Why not?

—Because they're partly responsible. There's a doorway – a portal – round here.

—What kind of doorway?

—An irregularity in the earth's magnetic field, a place where normal rules don't apply, that allows them to come and go—

—Come and go – where to?

—Iyama World, I suppose. Every time they use it, there's a burst of radiation. There's some research to suggest it was nuclear testing, back in the 1960s, that opened it up in the first place and let them in. They're using doorways of some kind, that's certain, probably over Bermuda. But now they think there's a new one.

—A new doorway?

Boney nodded. —That's why the area's thick with Iyama.

—They don't want another doorway?

Boney shook his head. —They're really rattled. It opened over the *Dayton* in a flash of light the other night, and now they think there's a leak.

—A leak?

—A doorway that isn't theirs.

—It wasn't a leak, it was *me*! Sinclair grew very excited. —It was when I arrived and went to Fish World, because I microwaved Daisy when I shouldn't have – *she's* a fish – and the microwave went BANG! He leapt up and clapped his hands. —And it was *me* arriving in F-F-Fish World, can't you *see*? And *you* were a fish in Fish World – he turned to Mr Davey— and now you're Mr *D – Davey* again—

—Davey? The tall man frowned. —My name's Abel Blamey.

—No, it isn't. Sinclair stopped dead. —You're Mr something Davey.

The tall man shook his head. —Abel Blamey. Itinerant preacher.

74

—Able Blame-me? What kind of a name is that?

—*My* name, Blamey said deeply.

—What's itinerant?

—Wandering.

—You're my R.E. teacher—

—I've never seen you before in my life.

—You teach R.E. in school—

—I think you'll find you're wrong.

—I'm not! Sinclair shouted, —you're Mr Davey!

—I'm not, said Abel Blamey.

Sinclair jumped up smartly.

—You *are* Mr Davey if I say you are!

—I think I'd know if I was.

Uncertain of anything since leaving the China House except that this was Mr Davey, this last frustration was too much for Sinclair Kuet.

—You are and don't say you're not!

—You've got me mixed up with someone else. Abel Blamey smiled. —I must be very like him.

—Sinclair, it doesn't matter. Alma looked upset.

Sinclair stamped his feet and howled in the way he sometimes did when he had to be calmed with his 'Sporting Howlers' video played over and over again.

—He *did* say his name was Abel Blamey, Mayo put in. —Maybe you better sit down.

—*I DON'T WANT TO SIT DOWN*! Sinclair lost his temper. Screaming at the top of his voice, he threw into a screech that hurt his throat all the anger and confusion he'd felt since leaving the world that he knew. —*YOU'RE MR DAVEY AND THAT'S WHO*

75

YOU ARE AND THAT'S WHAT REALLY YOUR
NAME IS!

—Please stop. Alma hugged him.

—Get off me! Sinclair struggled, but Alma only held him tighter. He panicked; felt trapped, then gave in. Alma held him closer; more securely.

—Please – be quiet – they'll send someone down, and then—

—What? Sinclair looked at her, struck by her mood.

—And then they'll take someone away.

Alma looked fearfully up at the hatch and the *taste* of the moment felt sinister, the way the feeling can change in a dream from okay to *not*-okay at the hint of something not-nice. Sinclair subsided, trembling all over, and several things fell into place – the strange-looking utensils in the kitchen – the acid in barrels – the hair that could've been a wig but could've been also *a scalp*, the flesh-trailing teeth in a bottle, *the scraps stuck on plates in the galley*—

Sinclair swallowed.

—So – Iyama – they're looking for *food*.

A special silence fell. A special knowledge filled every face.

Sinclair looked around him. Was there a suggestion that *they* – in the hold – might *be* the food?

—What is it? He spread his arms. —What is it, what did I say?

They all knew, but him.

But no one even tried to frame him an answer.

That night Sinclair sat down with a pen and the

back of the Captain's old notebook. Under the single tallow lantern his hand moved rapidly over the page, seemingly with no effort at all. He hummed as he drew, sometimes gazing at Alma, who had given herself up to quiet crying in the corner. She did that now and again. The tension was pretty unbearable. The ship's hold heaved and wallowed, and no one knew what would happen.

Sinclair looked down at his notebook, surprised, as ever, to see the network of lines.

—Did *you* draw that? Boney looked gobsmacked.

Sinclair nodded. He had.

The intricately-traced plan of the ship included, of course, no bits that he hadn't seen. But every single thing he *had* seen was represented in a spidery scrawl that respected scale and detail in such a way that the junk was clearly explained.

—That's amazing, Mayo breathed.

Sinclair shrugged. —I do buildings, mainly. Sometimes I like to do cars.

—How about people?

Sinclair shook his head. —I don't do people.

—We can't get out this way – Boney examined the plan – and we can't get out *this* way – we don't know what's next to the hold. And the hatch—

—We'll never get out, Sinclair said, taking his drawing back coolly.

Much later on, deep in the night, Sinclair awoke in a sweat. He jumped up and hopped the three steps to the hatch and battered on it with all his might.

—I WANT TO GET OUT! I WANT TO GET OUT! I WANT TO GET OUT, I DO!

Alma threw herself over him and brought him away and hugged him tight – too tight – until he fell uneasily asleep. The dream of his entry into Fish World returned to him in technicolour as half-sleeping, half-waking, he dozed off again. Dreams were weird, but *Run*, the sailor had said. *Run, it's the end of the world.* They'd beached the boat, and he – Sinclair – had seen people who snapped into monsters with shining red and green skins and dinosaur-spikes down their back – he remembered it now – now it was all coming back . . . now kindly Bob Ames was opening a tiny hatch and whispering between gleaming teeth . . . *It was for your own good, believe me . . . I had to shop you, shipmate . . . I'm sorry you had it hard in the hold . . . I had to do it to protect you . . . you're the one . . . don't you know . . . you have to rescue them all . . .*

A small hatch snapped shut. Had Robert Ames really spoken to him, or had in been a part of his dream? Sinclair sat up and became aware that he was slowly drowning in mist. He could see it slowly seeping in, smoking between the clinker-built boards, threading through all the hull and collecting, like snow, in the hold. Sinclair tried to touch it. It was the weirdest looking-mist he'd ever seen; the sort of mist pilots reported, just before they said everything looked kind of *milky* outside, and were never heard of again. He remembered what Boney, the Captain, had said . . . they were sailing into a portal, perhaps; entering a magnetic mahogany – anomaly – a place where normal rules didn't apply—

Sinclair drew in his feet as the mist rolled under the hatch and crept in spiralling curls across the floor; across Alma's mother's sleeping back; across Boney and Mayo; across the narrow back of Abel Blamey; across everyone asleep on the floor, spreading its mysterious influence with a whispered breath of strangeness and confusion.

The junk shuddered. There were shouts overhead.

—Hold your course! someone yelled. —Where are we? The water looks funny!

—Compass is going round like a top! I can't tell what the course *is*! someone else answered hectically.

Sinclair had known he was right. This was no ordinary mist. He considered the rapidly-disappearing hold, and the disappearing shapes on the floor. Should he shout? He'd better not. They'd go mad if he woke them again.

He tugged his jumper and coughed once or twice. He had strangest feeling *someone was throwing a net over him*. He felt as though he were trapped. Still the mist seeped in, and Sinclair began to enter a mood in which nothing very much seemed to matter, not even the questions which swarmed in his head like a whirling column of silver fish going round and round and round . . .

Alone in a weird mist, so what? *Was* it the end of the world? If so, *which* world? Where did Iyama come from? What was Iyama World like? What had that third flash been, the flash that had changed – and won – the Maser battle at sea? And where had Aunt Ping gone? *How could they see her face in the sky? How come her face* was *the sky?*

10

HUNKY AND NOT-NICE

Quite some time before Sinclair had got around to wondering how his Aunt Ping's face was the sky, and a little while before it *was* the sky, Aunt Ping and Dim Sum the cat had found themselves floating in a powder-blue universe, in orbit around a world that on closer inspection turned out to be a planet-sized blood-red rose.

There was no telling how long they'd orbited, or how long they *would* orbit, since time had seemed to stand still, since – since whenever it had stood still. Aunt Ping regarded the rose-world with something between astonishment and annoyance. She wouldn't have been surprised if it had decided to speak. Then she would have been able to tell it a thing or two. But the blood-red planet in a powder-blue universe had declined to do anything but revolve in a very grand manner, leaving Aunt Ping nothing to do but admire the fascinating display of its ever-opening petals as it very slowly revealed to her every side of what looked like, but couldn't be, a gorgeous damask rose.

Nothing would surprise her now. Although the

extremely strange landscape she found herself floating in right after the microwave banged in the old back kitchen was as inexplicable to Aunt Ping as an alien wandering in and ordering a curry, which in fact, unknown to Aunt Ping, had actually happened, as Iyama were everywhere – she had decided to *get used to it*. As far as Aunt Ping was concerned, she'd temporarily gone mad, and that was that. She'd never had a hallucination before in her life, but she supposed there was always a first time. Possibly it was too much ginseng. The funny thing was, the cat seemed to be having it with her. How many dreams or hallucinations included a floating cat?

What really worried her was the wok. Only moments before she'd gone mad she'd been tossing prawns, garlic, ginger, spring onion and bean sprouts together in a really hot wok on full flame on the stove. Wherever she was – whatever had happened – the prawns would be burning by now. In minutes the oil would ignite and a flame would shoot up and catch the extractor, then the strip-curtain, then the cardboard boxes on the side, then the matting on the floor, and the China House would burn down or be irreparably damaged by smoke in twenty minutes or less, not to mention the danger to the flat above, and it would be *all her fault* – unless she could somehow find Sinclair.

Despite her worries, the rose-world revolving in a perfect blue sky and growing very slightly closer every time she orbited it, distracted Aunt Ping in the way that being knocked down by a bus might have focused her attention. It distracted Dim Sum the cat. Aunt Ping reached over and stroked Dim Sum, who yawned and stretched luxuriously. Floating with a cat in a powder-blue universe – she would wake up soon, Aunt Ping hoped.

Meanwhile, she examined the rose. She could smell the scent of it now. Gorgeous ripe petals unfolded in slow motion, revealing indescribable shades of red between their folds, leading the watcher, it seemed, into an ever-deepening spiral into the heart of the flower. Aunt Ping held her breath. It was as if some giant secret were about to be disclosed. She could even see spots of dew trembling on outer petals, magnifying their blood-red veins and the insects that buzzed around them – or *were* they insects?

In fact, they were space-ships. Aunt Ping boggled; tiny, little space-ships, buzzing to and fro, along richly blood-red spirals which opened before them into deeper, more secret spirals – into the heart of the rose. If only she could see into it; but the unfolding heart of the rose was hidden from sight now by the landing platforms which jutted out between petals, and – oh! —Aunt Ping gasped; *whole cities* nestled beneath.

Still the rose opened before them. Now they were steering a course directly into the flower, sinking into and along a cool, dark well beneath petals the size of three continents. Aunt Ping swallowed. It was as if the Rose Planet *wanted* her and Dim Sum the cat. And they weren't they only ones. Behind them a long

83

wake of toasters, ships, trees, whales, chimneys, muffins, dustbins, spanners, traffic cones, supermarket trolleys, sheep, dentists, tube-trains and Masai tribesmen approached the slowly revolving World in a march of illogical objects.

There seemed to be something inevitable about it. The Rose Planet was *bringing them in*.

Closer and closer – now Aunt Ping could make out the texture of the petals, the perfume of which was overwhelming. Tiny, jewel-like monsters with glittering spines down their backs were visible everywhere on 'roadways' over the veined and textured surfaces opening before her. Aunt Ping gasped; there were thousands – millions – of them. What a strange way to live; what strange cities, nestling in blood-red darkness; what a strange world, with its lizard-things crawling all over it. It really beat everything. They looked like greenfly on their rose. She wouldn't have hesitated to spray them.

Darkness fell over Dim Sum the cat as they began the long descent into an endless dark well between petals. Aunt Ping wasn't comfortable with it – too late she saw the danger. Once sucked in by that perfect perfumed Rose Planet with its ever-opening heart and its cities and landing platforms and tiny green jewel-like monsters, *how would they ever come out*?

—Help! Aunt Ping cried, —save me! Sinclair – *turn off the wok*!

Dimly, as through a veil, she discerned a ship below her. Brilliant flashes of light lit up a stormy sea as a

second ship, rigged in purple, fired on the first. Aunt Ping put up her arms and tried to reach into the battle, but some thin membrane prevented her, as though she were caught in a bag. Somewhere down there was Sinclair. If only she could reach through.

—Help me! Aunt Ping cried. —Where am I? *Sinclair, are you there*?

In the last few seconds before the shadow of the Rose overwhelmed her, Aunt Ping felt as though she were pressing her face against that perfect, powder-blue sky. And suddenly Aunt Ping was looking *through* the sky, and down on the China House Takeaway.

She could actually hear the bell ding on the door as Monahan jogged in. Aunt Ping groaned; *Oh, no*. Mr Monahan, fitness freak and Inspector of Food, came in now and again to eat. At other times he came to inspect, and everything *better* be good. Running on the spot like a madman, Monahan considered the menu. He'd been down the gym since six, now he'd like Roast Duck with Beansprouts, King Prawns and Mushrooms and Young Chow Fried Rice, thank *you* very much.

Monahan looked around. The whole place smelled of burning. A pair of fried-looking shoes waited under a chair. 'Watchdog' blared on the telly. A copy of the *Sun* lay scattered around on the floor. Strange scorch marks lined the walls. A small terrier, tied to the leg of a chair, eyed him sadly behind it. It was seven o'clock, usually rush hour, but tonight for some reason the China House Takeaway – empty of Aunt Ping, empty of customers, empty of everyone but Daisy the fish, very slightly microwaved, who swam round and round in her tank – looked as though a bomb had hit it. Sinclair's order book lay open on the counter. It was a real *Marie Celeste* job – a deserted shop, instead of a deserted ship. Funny, funny, funny. Very funny indeed. For a moment Monahan wondered if the China House was open, or if he'd got the wrong day or the wrong time or the wrong idea or the wrong street or something. Then he knew he hadn't. Wasn't he always right? Where was everybody? What did you have to do to get some service here?

—Shop! Anyone there? I'd like to order while I'm young! Monahan peered over the counter, but nothing came out of the kitchen but a gathering pall of smoke.

Monahan acted quickly, to give him his due. Although bulky and chiselled-looking in an 'Ice Warriors' kind of way, with impressive pecs and an arrogance problem – what Sinclair called hunky-and-*not*-nice – he could move pretty swiftly if he had to. Hurdling the counter, he fenced his way into the smoking kitchen with the legs of a chair, located the smoking wok first time, and hurled it out of the window. He turned off the gas and shook out a fire blanket over the smouldering stove. He threw open the skylight and both tiny windows, scattering the bottles of relish lining the sills with his meaty arms. He doused the sink in water and swept up the smoking remains of hessian matting and sodden cardboard boxes on the floor.

After a while the smoke cleared. Monahan shouted up the garden.—*Hello? Anyone there?* Then he put the kettle on and made himself a cup of tea. He put his feet up and drank it. Monahan was quite a hero.

After a while he felt peckish. He looked around the kitchen. The scene of recent damage had been concentrated near the stove. Near the microwave by the strip curtain a meal, evidently To Go, awaited collection. Monahan looked in the box. He lifted the lids on the foil containers and sniffed. Prawns Sweet & Sour, Chicken Fried Rice, Spare Ribs and – Pancakes with Maple Syrup, a new idea from Cousin Sang, who had visited the States on holiday and become addicted to pancakes overnight. Monahan felt drool welling up, even though the dishes were cold. The Kuets owed him their takeaway. They wouldn't begrudge him a meal.

Monahan piled food onto a plate.

Slipping in the spare ribs to start with, then making room for reheated pancakes as well, Monahan stabbed 'cook' on the grease-splattered microwave by the strip curtain. He settled back to wait three mins. Microwaves were a grand invention. He could hear those spare ribs hissing now. Talk, you beauties, talk. In fact, they were hissing too much. Woh – flashing as well – probably he'd better turn them over – did this microwave *usually* bang?

The last thing Michael Monahan, Inspector of Food, could clearly remember doing in the kitchen of the China House Takeaway, High St, Wortham, that night, was taking a fork out of the cutlery drawer to turn his spare ribs over.

The rest was a mighty bang and a flash of light.

And a pair of smoking trainers, exactly Monahan's size, exactly where Monahan had left them, exactly in front of the microwave, which dinged after exactly three minutes.

11

NEW PORK

At the very moment Sinclair was speculating how horrified she'd be at the thought of Iyama soup with red-and-blue spines swimming in it during the argument with Alma on the *Annaho*, Mae Ling finished her Iyama steak, wiped her mouth, and handed the rest to the pigs in Central Park. She burped contentedly. Whatever Iyama *was*, it wasn't half-bad.

She looked around – where next? 'Central Park Children's Zoo' a crooked sign announced. The larch-lap gates stood open and mossy-looking, as if they'd stood open for years. Somewhere inside them something was screaming with rage. Even the nearest large porker raised its head as a family of chimps dashed out, one of them chasing the rest with bared teeth, tearing up and throwing clumps of grass, then running up a tree and throwing sticks down in a rage. Temper, temper. Mae Ling giggled. Animals ran the park, she guessed; suppose they ran everything else? She looked around more observantly. Animals were everywhere. A bunch of noisy racoons descended on trash-cans nearby; prairie dogs popped up in a complicated system of burrows that criss-crossed between paths; parrots screeched in the tree-tops. Mae Ling got up, bemused. Looks like the zoo got out, she thought. Looks like *we're* in the zoo.

Lazily, Mae Ling wandered out of the park and down Fifth Avenue. Turtle Bay St, Woodchuck St, Cow St, Pig St, Duck St – roads intersecting Fifth Avenue once numbered 55th, 54th, 53rd street were all now named for animals, Mae Ling noticed. Was this New York, or a *version* of New York, like the bus-boy calling himself Redmond who seemed to be a *version* of Kevin Lee – New York, but not New York?

Mae Ling wandered on in the sunshine. Everywhere streets hummed with pig-smells; Exhibition Cows exhibited themselves in the sunshine – on street-corners, in shop doorways – even in the Rockefeller Center, where restaurant tables had been moved to make room for a hefty Friesian who had wanted to collapse near the fountains. In the fountains seals lazed, clapping themselves now and then for being so stylish as to shop there. Sheep grazed on any and every knot of grass, and in every park; escaped iguanas dozed on car-bonnets; flocks of screaming parakeets and squirrels threw down debris from roof-gardens; monkeys hung in the phone lines; chickens scratched a living in Macy's department store; horses grazed restaurants for sugar cubes and banks for complimentary mints; black bears nudged over fruit stalls and nosed in the spinning melons; guinea pigs flocked in gutters and everywhere hamsters ran wild. Cool, Mae Ling thought, all-*right*. Animals Rool, OK.

But it wasn't *all* OK. Desperate-looking people begged for coins in vain as shoppers pampered pigeons with pecans, pretzels and pumpernickel bread. Buskers played for a dime, while next to them cows lay down on sandwich stalls and toppled urns of coffee. Spoiled little dogs in velvet coats minced along past thrift shops; cats crossed roads unhurriedly and brought taxis screeching to a halt – there was even a CAT CROSSING sign at every set of lights under WALK – DON'T WALK. Mae Ling knitted her brows. How could this be OK? Even the Trump Tower had pigs in its entrance foyer. Mae Ling shook her head at the very absurd sight of businesswomen stepping over them in court shoes. Why in the Veggie World didn't someone throw them out?

The Sweepers were something else. Following a bunch of uniformed boys earnestly sweeping the streets with wide-headed brushes, Mae Ling turned in at a giant slab which had to be the Empire State Building.

—Excuse me – what are you doing?

The Official State Sweeper tipped his hat. — Sweeping for life-forms. Watch your step, please.

Mae Ling jumped. The Sweeper bent, then squinted. He held up something infinitesimal between his fingers.

—Saskatchewan Street Mite—

—I'm sorry?

—Statutory fine thirty dollars—

—Statutory *fine*?

—so we don't wanna crush one of *those* babies.

Elbowing open a jar from his trolley, he dropped in the invisible street mite.

Mae Ling cleared her throat.

—Is this the Empire State Building, or what?

The State Sweeper regarded her sadly. He pointed to a sign inside the building's marble lobby which read: 'Neils Christian Haansen Votive Sheep Tower. Queue Here For Observatory.' Under the sign the end of a long queue was visible snaking around a corner.

—Oh! Mae Ling said. —Thanks.

—You're welcome. Have a mice day. The Official State Sweeper swept on.

Mae Ling joined the queue. She waited and waited and waited. What was the hold-up here? The people in front of her were German so she couldn't understand what they said, but the things they were saying in German were *sounding* pretty impatient – when at last the queue moved on. When Mae Ling got round the corner she found a sheep had got trapped in a turnstile. Finally security men wrenched it bodily upwards and out as its bleating filled the long marble halls and several people tutted at such cruelty and decided they might go and brush squirrels instead. The smell of lanolin from the sheep filling the lift made Mae Ling's head spin. She popped out all the same on the 86th floor observatory to find animals' New York spread below her.

The haze in the distance covered Liberty too well for Mae Ling to see her properly.

—Could I? —Thanks.

Borrowing a friendly woman's binoculars, Mae Ling scanned the horizon; finally – there she was! The Statue of Liberty, looming in the haze with her half-secret smile and her bold chin and her aquiline nose and her blue-green robes and her arm thrust inspiringly upwards holding a—

Mae Ling lowered the bins. —Did Liberty always have an eagle?

The woman nodded. —Always.

—But I thought she carried a torch.

—Never a torch. Always an eagle.

—Right.

Mae Ling looked beneath her, where Broadway made the only diagonal line on the chequerboard that was Manhattan. Using the bins, she traced a line of roof-gardens where *horses* seemed to be grazing. Interesting . . . away in the north-east, beyond the flashing cap of the Chrysler Building and far away out beyond Queens, a line of *really big* factory units of some sort threw back the light from the—

—Offerings here! Pellets, barley, greens!

Dodging the sheep crowding the viewing platform, Mae Ling approached the boy with a tray of what could have been sweets.

—Get your votives here! Pellets, barley—

—Got any ice-cream? she asked him.

—Jessica? the boy with the tray wrinkled his nose. 'Approved Vendor, N. C. H. Votive Sheep Tower', read the badge on his lapel.

—No, Mae Ling said coldly.

—You're *not* Jessica?

—Got it in one. Do you have any ice-creams?

He wrinkled his nose again. —Boy, you look just like her. You *sure* you—

—My name's Mae Ling. Ices.

—We don't sell ice-cream.

—What, then?

He put his head on one side. Who did he think she was? It was, Mae Ling saw in a flash, a *Kevin Lee situation* – or a Kevin Lee Reversal, as she would call it – only *the other way round*, this time. How many worlds intersected, here? Two, or maybe three?

She held up a packet of herb-like stuff. —So, she said, —what are these?

—Today we have barley, campion, fresh meadow-grass—

—Yes, but what *for*?

He looked at her blankly. —To offer?

—Offer where?

But suddenly Mae Ling saw where. All along the mesh fence people were offering grass: shaking out little packets into the breeze which carried it over New York, or New *Pork*, as it probably called itself by now. So this tower commemorated sheep. So you bought grass and 'offered' it to them. No wonder the nearest roof gardens were stiff with a layer of hay.

The boy with the tray shook his head again.

—You *sure* you're not Jess—

—Say it again, I'll deck you.

—Hey. He put up his arms. —No problem. He moved away with his little bags of greens, still convinced, Mae Ling could see, that she was Jessica someone-or-other, probably Jessica slightly-better-looking or Jessica slightly-more-slim. So what. Deal with it, Mae.

Rejoining her lady with the binoculars, Mae Ling considered the view over the East River. But again her eyes were drawn downwards. Beneath on the swarming streets the animals weren't so visible. That this was their city wasn't so obvious now, as Mae Ling looked down on taxi-cabs riddling the streets like maggots between huge luxury triple-decker buses, the kind she'd seen on the rank, when she'd first spotted Kevin/Redmond.

She tried to count the different kinds. Orange and black tops-of-buses crawled between red-and-gold ones – Imperials, weren't they? Or Corinthians. No – Corinthian buses were blue and white – there! On Sixth Avenue! One; two – three Corinthian Line buses, and over on Seventh, a fourth; and crawling up Broadway, one behind another like cough lozenges, two green-and-gold Holden Line buses and a Town & Country Line Topper in lickety-split stripes of maroon and white. Between them wandered Exhibition Cows. Why didn't they get run over?

—How far do those big buses *go*? Mae Ling wondered aloud.

—All the way upstate. The friendly woman with the binoculars shrugged. —Depends how far you wanna go.

—All the way out to *those*? Mae Ling pointed to the huge and sinister-looking factory units lining the horizon. —What are they, anyway?

—Iyama farm.

—Excuse me?

—What I said. Iyama farm. They're in the city, too.

—Iyama's a meat substitute, right?

—Say what?

—Don't you have tofu or soya-protein? That's what Iyama is, right?

—Whatever. The woman looked at her strangely, not so friendly now.

—*Because this is Veggie World, right, and no one kills anything*, Mae Ling whispered to herself, looking down on the Exhibition Cows.

Out in the farm-smelling traffic again, between poo-piles left by horses, Mae Ling found herself following the bus routes to see if one of them carried Kevin Lee-who-called-himself-Redmond. Kevin/Redmond was her only link with anything remotely connected with reality. He had to know where Sinclair was – hadn't he been in the Takeaway just before they'd all flashed away and everything had gone freaky?

Following a Balment Line Topper flashed with black

and orange, Mae Ling threaded dingy streets. Shops chocked with rolls of fabric in horrible colours gave way to SuperPizza and Big Iyamaburger. Dodging a line of squealing pigs streaming out of a warehouse ahead of her, Mae Ling entered a street where the giant bus was forced to squeeze between parked delivery vehicles. The noise was incredible as things were loaded and unloaded, lorry sides bashed with large items, warehouse doors rolled up and down, and orders bawled and contradicted. Behind it all the not-so-distant wail of police sirens and the nearby sound of a road drill and the panicked squeals of the pigs made a soundtrack for any third ring of hell, had anyone known what it was.

Mae Ling pushed through determinedly. She would make sense of this if she had to kill herself running. If she couldn't actually catch up with the bus, she would follow it back to the rank and wait and watch for Kevin/Redmond. She ran, then walked, then ran again. She could have practically hopped on to the stupid bus, if only that stupid silver van wasn't totally in the way. The slogan on the back of it was a puzzler:

Primrose Meadow Farms – Your First Stop for Fresh Iyama

steaks – breast – leg joints – brisket – tail – liver

This was Veggie World – what could 'leg' joints be? Why were *tails* advertised? What on earth was brisket? Puzzled, Mae Ling slowed. At that particular moment, a sonorous clashing and banging drew her attention. Passing the warehouse now, she glanced inside.

Inside the warehouse on the streets of New Pork, a sight met Mae Ling's eyes that defied explanation and chilled her blood and made her feel sick to her stomach. Something large and green and *alligator*-looking hung in rows in the darkened warehouse, like pigs on a butcher's hook. They weren't pigs. They weren't alligators. They weren't dinosaurs, although a bit like them. The slowly-revolving carcasses in the warehouse were *unlike anything she'd ever seen before in her life*. Mae Ling stared in disbelief. Their thick tails trailed on the floor. Their brown blood collected in pools. Their broken necks hung at funny angles. Their glazed eyes looked blankly out at her. Their red and blue spines wilted down.

Mae Ling's heart hammered. What-*are*-they-What-*are*-they-What-*are*-they? Someone had to know.

—What – what is that? she asked Primrose Meadows truck driver faintly.

—This? Main distribution unit for the best Iyama in the world – hey, you all right?

Mae Ling backed away. The green reptilian corpses swayed very slightly as someone rolled down the door.

There could be no doubt they were dead. There could be no doubt someone had killed them. There could be no doubt they were creatures – whatever kind of creatures they *were*. And *this* was Veggie World? *Where she'd eaten battered Iyama?*

Mae Ling felt her world fall away. She felt like throwing up. The pavement looked dirty; the shops, the street – even the sky looked dirty.

Covering her mouth, Mae Ling ran. And ran and ran and ran, she didn't know where.

12

BOB AMES EXPLAINS

A puff of mist rolled on the water. Out of it suddenly
burst a junk, its spars heavy with Iyama, already
reefing her sails as she shot, like a dart, into port. The
lights of 42nd Street, now Forty Camels Street, shone
beyond and behind her in the night sky, and beyond
them the Neils Christian Haanson Votive Sheep
Tower threw up it's floodlights to a moon with a
monkey's face. The approaching junk slipped silently
in and Animal City slept on, not knowing, not caring,
about the tick that had landed to annoy it, and all its
lights blazed down. It was a sight to take your breath
away. The city glittered on the water like a jewel, as
the junk *Annaho* reefed her sails and put in at the
Circle Line dock.

Not that Sinclair could see it.

Down in the hold, all was darkness and queasiness
and strange shouts and sudden noises. *Annaho* heaved
uneasily as her hull nudged Pier Seventeen. Hawsers
snaked over the deck and whipped through pulleys.
Seamen shouted overhead. The anchor plummeted
down like a dead man.

Sinclair shook Alma. She wouldn't wake up. He shook her again and again.

—We're docking, he told her. —This is it.

Alma woke miserably and shook the others.

—We're here! Come on – get up!

The men and women and children in the hold of the *Annaho* stirred leaden limbs and stretched and tried to get up. They'd been a long time in the mist asleep. Only Sinclair knew how long.

Suddenly a little hatch snapped back and some gleaming teeth appeared.

—Shipmates, whispered the gleaming teeth, —will you take your chance with Bob Ames?

Sinclair cleared his throat.

—That depends, he said.

The teeth grew more confidential. —I says to myself, they'll understand when Bob Ames had to give them up when he found himself in a tightish place, or do them no good in the future.

Sinclair wasn't having it. —So you *had* to tell them where we were?

—Napes would have sniffed you out. Bob Ames'll see you right in the end, if he goes a strange way about it.

—Why should we trust you? Alma said.

—There ain't much time, the teeth replied. —But if you'll run when Bob Ames tips you the wink, you'll get clean away before they notice.

The tiny hatch snapped shut as suddenly as it had opened.

A few seconds later the main hatch shifted quietly, and Sinclair climbed the steps and emerged into a version of his dream, only strangely twisted. Instead of a little boat on a night sea, he had the heaving deck of a junk unloading its cargo stealthily under the moon. Instead of phosphorescent Fish World under his bows, he had the glittering reflection of the city in all its irridescent clothes. Instead of a fisherman to rescue him, he had Bob Ames. But still the feeling of danger never left him.

One by one, the survivors of the *Dayton Ohio* slipped out of the hold and concealed themselves on the cargo deck, some muffling children, some blinking and staring, some quick, some slow; all afraid. Some huddled with Boney; others streamed immediately over the quays and were swallowed up in the darkness.

Bob Ames shook his head. —They won't get far, he said.

—Why not? Sinclair asked him.

—It's the Taint – they'll drop in their boots before midnight.

—The Taint?

—Too long with Iyama, like.

—You mean – too long eating not-real food?

—And the rest. Bob Ames sniffed. —Smell 'em?

Sinclair smelled the survivors on the wind. It was true. They smelled of metal.

—Take these lemons. Ames opened a kit-bag yellow with fruit. —They're real – no Iyama rubbish. He

103

urged the bag on Sinclair. —Rub 'em over your skin. Tell the others to do it.

Sinclair felt ill. —Am *I* tainted, too?

—No, you're clear as a bell. Robert Ames looked at him. —I was tainted to the hilt once, myself – now you see me as I am.

As I am. Sinclair looked at him. *What are you?* he wanted to ask.

Robert Ames laid his hands on Sinclair's shoulders, as serious as he was likely to ever get.

—If there's others here like you, find them and take them back with you. People you know – that you recognise. It's up to you to rescue them. Always stick by your shipmates – a promise is a promise to Bob Ames – what d'you say?

Robert Ames' words rang in Sinclair's head. Mr Davey, or Abel Blamey, as he insisted on calling himself – where was he? What about Napes/David Selwyn? *Always stick by your shipmates – a promise is a promise* – Easy to say, but how was he going to get back with them? The same way, he supposed, they got in.

—Well?

Sinclair nodded. —I promise.

Behind Robert Ames skyscrapers reared up into the night sky, crowning his head with their lights. Beyond them illuminated bridges hung like necklaces over the river. Sinclair caught his breath as the city looked down like a diamond.

—Where is this place? Sinclair breathed.

—A city we've jumped to.

—By magnetism?

—You're a sharp one, Robert Ames said.

It was wonderful; magical; incredible. The night air and the growl of the streets bit into Sinclair's heart with a flavour he would never forget. Someday he would draw this night city. He would get every detail right.

He looked up at Robert Ames, the lights shining through his beard and moustache, his careful face watching and waiting for the moment to tip them the wink, his lively brown eyes scouting the decks for the moment to make their escape, and knew him, in that moment, for a friend. Sinclair nodded at the swarming Iyama attending to a hundred different tasks, swiftly and silently docking their ship under the nose of their enemies – he *supposed* their enemies. Who was at the bottom of whose food-chain? It was all mixed up in Sinclair's mind with the horrible crusty old pretend food he'd been living off down in the hold, the chemicals he'd glimpsed in the galley, and the way no one would tell him anything, as if there was some big secret which was probably that Iyama ate people, but then people ate Iyama and *that* was no secret, and he was tired and fed up with it all, anyway—

—Iyama – why are they here?

Robert Ames laughed grimly. —Revenge, he said, —that's what for.

—Revenge?

—They've been planning this for a long time.

—Please explain, Sinclair said.

—I don't know the whys or the wherefores, Robert Ames began. —But I think things reached a head, you might say, when Iyama came in accidentally through 'holes' in the earth's magnetic field, a bit like the one we've just sailed through—

—They're strange, Sinclair said. —I don't like them – especially the mist.

—They came through, as I say, at least in the beginning, with the jolliest and best intentions, exploring – *prospecting*, if you like. But what d'you say to an alien saying 'hello' to you one morning, with his green skin all bright and shining and his tail hanging over his arm?

Sinclair thought. —I'd be scared.

—Exactly right. People were scared of Iyama, and when people get scared all sorts of good things like friendship and trust and the rest of it, well, they go to the dogs. And people arm themselves – and the next thing, you've got a war on.

Sinclair had to admit he was right. That was probably *exactly* what would happen.

—Well, governments get themselves in a twist, and the next thing it's shoot on sight. And poor old Iyama get bundled away and shot and fried and, oh – all manner of sights you don't want to see, nor Bob Ames to tell you about.

—Then what? Sinclair looked glum.

—Oho, then we find they're good meat.

—Good meat?

—Good eating, Bob Ames explained. —Iyama steak; Iyamaburger; battered Iyama, refried Iyama sandwich, roast Iyama, Iyama fricasse, Italian Iyama bake—

—All right, Sinclair said. —What next?

—Ah, that's the plum on the cake. What happens next, if you *like* to be beat with your own stick, I should say was the best of it.

—What do you mean?

—What happens next is Mr Iyama goes and takes a leaf of our book, thank *you* very much – and just like your native Americans learned scalping from white men, who scalped *them* first, your Iyama takes a tip from the kindly race he's bumped into and very soon starts—

—*Eating us.* Sinclair's face whitened. —They eat us, as well – *don't they?*

—I don't say they do, I don't say they don't. But I *do* say we make our move soon.

Robert Ames scanned the deck.

Sinclair put a few things together himself. It wasn't so different to a maths problem. —And they don't want the *Dayton Ohio* monitoring radiation, because they don't want their doorways discovered – and then suddenly, bang! —*we* come in—

—Stow it, shipmate. Robert Ames hushed him urgently.

Sinclair saw the danger. Already Iyama were hauling cargo. Soon they would approach their hiding place. Already the deck shook under them whenever a cargo block moved.

—Hadn't we better go now?

—Soon. Bob Ames held Sinclair back. Cannily he watched the line of Iyama unloading the cargo bays and streaming in regular lines up several gangplanks. The cycle moved around like clockwork, and one of its movements had all heads down at once, and that was the moment to move.

—So they're here for revenge? Sinclair murmured. Poor Iyama. It wasn't their fault, after all. Probably they were cuddly, if you let them be. They didn't *look* very cuddly.

—They're here to burn down houses and torch humanity and to make an end of the world, since people don't care for them much, and now – *now*! Robert Ames sprang up, spying all heads down at once. —*Now or never – run*!

Sinclair rose, blinking.

Giving him a mighty push, Robert Ames windmilled his arms. —Go now! All of you! Run – *before it's too late*!

Before he knew it Sinclair had grabbed Alma's arm and leapt one of several gangplanks to the quay, with a rush of feet behind him so hot at his heels, whether friend or Iyama, he didn't stop to see. A sense of panic gripped him. *Run, it's the end of the world!*

Iyama caught up with hawsers could only watch their escape. Others drew Masers reluctantly, prepared to let some of them go before drawing unwelcome attention to the silent docking of the *Annaho*. Sinclair only looked back once, and that was to see Robert

Ames go up in a sheet of flame, his windmilling arms trying in vain to hold back the single Maser-bolt which lit up the night sky like lightning.

Then he turned for his life and ran like a mad thing, sensing dark obstacles a split-second before hurdling them, down streets with startled dogs and trash cans bowling, past tramps surprised around burning tyres, past horses drowsing on corners, past night-owls booming in trees and foxes out on the prowl and over and under and through a children's playground, with the moonlight glinting off the swings and pigs asleep in the sand.

Alma bounded past him. He caught her up and ran madly between two shadows and into an alley so close and so densely dark he might have been blinded or dead.

—Wait! he sobbed. —Please wait!

In fact, he *was* half-blinded. Alma came to him and held him.

—Did you look at the Maser-bolt?

Sinclair nodded miserably.

—Never look at a Maser-bolt. Never mind. Blink a lot. It'll wear off in a minute.

Sinclair blinked a lot and colours swam in front of his eyes. The distant sounds of shouting and running feet had died away. Once again he and Alma were out on their own – out in a city of lights and shadows, with everyone scattered everywhere and everything in a mess.

—I want Aunt Ping, he said.

—Never mind Aunt Ping. We're lucky to get away.

—Did you see – they shot him with flames—

Alma hugged him tighter.

—they b-burned him – burned him right up!

—You liked him, didn't you?

—They didn't – have to – *k–kill* him.

—They didn't, but they did.

—I *hate* those things.

—That's what they're like.

—I want to go home, Sinclair said.

Alma got up. —I'm going to find Mum now, she said.

—Can I come with you? Sinclair felt utterly miserable.

—They'll be watching – following – us. You'll be better off on your own.

—No, I'll be better with you.

—I'll meet you in three days' time, but watch out – something's going to happen.

—What?

Alma shuddered. —Iyama.

Sinclair watched her go. Then he shouted. —*Where?*

Alma turned.

—Lions Square.

—Where's Lions Square?

—You'll find out.

The only thing Sinclair knew was that he was alone and friendless in a huge, great unwelcoming city with a party of aliens after him like poison and nowhere – at all – to go.

—Please don't leave me, he whimpered.—*Alma, please come back*.

How could she leave him?

But Alma had gone. It was every man for himself.

Exactly three streets further on – on Bucephalus Square, to be precise – a gang of monkey-catchers were out for strays with a net. There were eight in the press gang plus Parky, and all of them were suck-ups and did what he told them and jumped when Parky said jump, and pulled up their socks when he told them to, and brushed their uniforms every night and told him just whatever he wanted to hear, because Parky was boss of the bus rank and everyone who helped net more bus-boys could help themselves to a bonus.

With the boss that night were Redmond, Radclyffe, Wolfie, Evian, Woodstock, Pomfret and Palfrey. Sciacallo, whose name meant Jackal, had tagged along.

Two streets away by now, Sinclair's footsteps rang out in the Animal City, where no-one padded by night but bears and raccoons and press gangs up to no good.

—Won't catch anything tonight. Pomfret spat. — Looks like the moon's too good.

The distant howl of a wolf belled between tenement blocks.

—Don't be too sure, Parky said, sniffing the air like a wolf himself, and not one in sheep's clothing, either.

A moment of tension passed; then *slip-slap* out of

the distance, only a street away now, Sinclair's footsteps announced him as well as a fanfare with lights.

Slip-slap, slip-slap—

—Hear that? Parky smiled. —There's one coming now.

Slip-slap, slip-slap – squeak—

—He's making the corner – get ready. Parky knew the squeak of a pair of boys' trainers on a city street as well as he knew his own pager.

—Can I? squeaked a boy named Radclyffe. —Please, Mr Parker, can I do it?

—Me, Mr Parker, said Redmond/Kevin Lee. —He did the last one, remember?

—This is a job for the big boys. Parky adjusted his net. —Shut it, will you, both of you – let me have some room.

Sinclair walked on in the moonlight, down street after street all the same, locked in a maze of misery, wanting, above all things, his bedroom, his drawing-pad, his art-box, his pencil-case and his mother, in that order.

Leaving Water Moccasin Street behind him, he turned on to Bucephalus Square, and his steps rang out in the moonlight.

—Brace yourselves, boys, Parky whispered.

13

NABBED!

His fish senses almost saved him. Feeling strange movements of air pressure over the lateral lines running down his sides, Sinclair paused uneasily on the corner of Bucephalus and Springbok and let his fish senses taste the air. He ducked across the rain-soaked square and emerged on the other side. He looked around him. Nothing. The statue of a riderless horse in the centre of the square either commemorated a brave horse, or the rider had got lost somewhere. Sinclair dug his hands in his pockets. He had to keep moving or freeze. Ahead of him a dreary perspective of streets opened out off the square, all of them named after animals. Next was Coyote Street.

Coyote Street was narrow and dark, and the corner with it was sharp. In a moment Sinclair crossed the street; in a moment the trap was sprung in the shadows on the other side; in a moment a net fell out of the sky; in a moment Parky was on him.

—Wait – no! —*get off me!*

—Quiet down, son – you're nabbed!

Sinclair fought like a tiger, but the net which

trapped and blinded him left him no room to move. Instantly arms weighed him down. Trussed like a chicken in moments, he was indeed thoroughly nabbed; the only part of him he could move was his eyelids, and under them the moon showed him someone leering down at him through the grid of the net, someone he knew quite well—

—Mr Monahan!

—Name and age? Parky waited.

—Mr Monahan – the Food Inspector! W-what are *you* doing here?

—All right then, name and age later. Parky/Monahan rose to his full height and straightened his iron-grey uniform. —The name's R. A. C. Parker, Recruitment, Buslink Bus Boys Incorporated. I have to inform you of your rights—

—What rights? someone shouted.

—which I'll be doing later. That's all you need to know for the moment, except—

—You're recruited, dork, someone yelled.

Parky put his face in Sinclair's – that from this moment on, you're mine.

Sinclair swallowed. Was he?

Parky smiled grimly. —What do you think about *that*?

Sinclair stared. Like David Selwyn – like Mr Davey, Monahan had *forgotten who he was*. He'd never liked Mr Monahan. Now he could suddenly see why. Just as suddenly he spotted Kevin Lee and the blood rushed up into his face.

—K – Kevin Lee, it's me, Sinclair – why are *you* here?

Redmond turned on him furiously. —I'm not Kevin stupid Lee, don't *ever* stupid call me it *again*.

—Do you know this boy? Parky asked Redmond icily.

—No, Mr Parker, I never even saw him before, it's just, I keep meeting people who call me Kevin Lee—

—Was it Mae Ling?

—You what?

—Mmmae L-Ling. Sinclair could hardly spit it out. —Was it a Chinese girl who called you Kevin Lee?

—Matter of fact, it was.

Sinclair's heart hammered. So Mae Ling had followed him here; somewhere, not far off, she was waiting.

Parky picked Redmond up by his collar. —I-said-do-you-know-this-boy?

—No, Mr Parker, honest.

—That's good. Parky put Redmond down and dusted off his jacket. —Because if you did, we'd have to lose him. Dismissing Redmond, he clapped his hands. —All right boys, a good night's work—

—And anyway, a small voice insisted, —I'm not yours, I'm *mine*.

—We'll see about that. Parky rounded on Sinclair. Then he smiled. —Take him away. I like 'em with a bit of spirit. Nothing wrong in that.

—You're a bus-monkey now, okay, and you're coming with us. A large boy with heavy eyebrows stripped Sinclair out of his net and hustled him into a van. —Wise up, stupid, he added, softly. —Don't rile him more than you have to.

—What's your name?

—Wolfie.

The street-lights showed Sinclair a boy not much older than himself with bad teeth and bad hair and a half-undone red uniform stiff with braid.

—How do I get away?

—You don't. There's worse jobs than being a bus monkey. I've been a Sweeper *and* a Sewer Rat. Wolfie smiled too brightly. —*Deal* with it, okay?

—That's the way – we'll rub along fine. Parky took the driver's seat. —We all look after each other on the rank, don't we, boys – what d'you say?

—Hoo! Radclyffe whistled. —You better believe it!

But Sinclair didn't believe it. Monahan's eyes were cold in his driving mirror, constantly checking him out. Who was he, really? Food Inspector? Boss of the bus rank? A caring human being, or some version of a caring human being? Something was wrong here – didn't these people have homes to go to? What did bus monkeys do?

Nodding along in the back of a van with a bunch of people he didn't know, through the animal-haunted streets to some unknown destination, some unknown fate in an unknown world he'd been in long enough to know wasn't all plain sailing, with the only person he recognised – someone he'd have to save to live up to the promise he'd made to his friend Robert Ames

– Sinclair felt he was entering withdrawal, which he sometimes stayed in for days. He hugged his knees in distress and rocked from side to side.

—Get out of the road, you ugly mug!

Parky sounded his horn and a large brown bear turned eyes like lamps towards them, then rolled unhurriedly away.

—They ought to shoot those bears – been on a bear-shoot, have you?

—Hunting's illegal, Mr Parker, Wolfie answered dutifully.

—So what? Boy Radclyffe sniggered.

Sinclair watched rodents scatter as Parky took the bends. Where were everyone's cars in this city? On the streets where there were parked cars, bands of monkeys had stripped them clean of anything detachable and left hub-caps, radio aerials and windscreen wipers lying in the road. They actually surprised some woolly monkeys peeling off windscreen trim like long strings of liquorice.

The blocks flickered by and Sinclair put his head between his knees and tried to make it all go away. Now *he* was a monkey, too, whatever that meant. It was a jungle out there. Inside was a jungle, too. *Always stick by your ship-mates*, Robert Ames had said. *It's up to you to save everyone. Promise you'll do that for me.* Bob Ames with his kindly voice and his searching eyes; Bob Ames who'd laid down his life so that he and Alma could escape. Sinclair welled up with tears. He was *feeling* something – what did it mean?

—All right, there? Parky adjusted his mirror. — How's the new boy going?

—All right, Mr Parker, thank you, Wolfie piped up for Sinclair. He rolled his eyes at Sinclair to show he was humouring the boss. It was pathetic he even bothered. How sad are *you*, Sinclair wondered.

—That's the way. Parky showed his teeth in an ugly smile. —We'll soon have you SHEDed up.

—What's SHED? Sinclair asked.

—Were you just *born*, or something? Redmond sniggered.

—Leave it, Redmond, Parky warned. Then he smiled again. —Lucky we bumped into you. Wolves around this time of night.

Sinclair felt the warning creep through his heart. Parky was sinister and grim and he'd promised to save him for Robert Ames's sake. Whatever Monahan called himself now, he was just the same bunch of muscles in a shirt he'd been as a Food Inspector, and his stupid Buslink uniform with its badge saying 'R.A.C. Parker, Manager' and the stupid tassels and epaulettes everywhere over his shoulders like spaghetti didn't make him any different to the no-brain who'd ordered Aunt Ping's pans destroyed and her every kitchen crevice cleaned with bleach, over and over again or she'd get closed down, when everyone *knew* the chippie down the road got off with a clean bill of health because Monahan's niece was the owner, surprise, surprise—

—Chocolate? offered Wolfie.

119

—Thanks. Sinclair took some. As he unwrapped it, he noticed it was called HED – no, SHED – it better be good, he thought, after they talked it up so much.

It *was* good – in a way. Sinclair chewed and chewed. It was pretty chewy chocolate, with toffee or something in the middle. It took an age to get rid of; probably about four blocks had slipped by, by the time he swallowed the end of it. A strange taste flooded his mouth. Pretty soon he felt good about himself. What was he worrying about? He could handle anything these guys could dish out. Nothing was going to phase him. Pretty soon he didn't care where he was going or who he was going there with. He didn't care what day it was or what any of them were doing there, or where he came from or what might happen to him at any time other than this.

At last Parky pulled in somewhere.

—What? Sinclair jumped.

—This is it, Wolfie repeated.

Sinclair watched, as if from a great height, as they stepped out on to the bus rank under the halogen security lights, where uniformed bus monkeys, all small boys like Sinclair himself, spilled out of the wheel-locked luxury Topper buses to examine the latest recruit who would meet-and-greet passengers like they did and be tied to his bus for life, or until he was thirteen and Parky had to pay him properly, whichever was the soonest.

—His name's Sinclair. Redmond pushed Sinclair forward and made him stand on a tyre.

—Edgecumbe, Parky corrected. —I've decided we'll call him Edgecumbe – unless anyone objects?

He looked around in a challenging way.

—The other Edgecumbe got dragged, Wolfie hissed. —You're his replacement, see?

—Dragged? Sinclair could just about be bothered to ask.

—Caught in his own bus doors, dragged two stops, completely shredded. His birthday, too. It happens. He would've been thirteen.

Wolfie shut up as Parky's eyes rested on him.

—I've changed my mind, Parky said steadily. — We'll call him Aldebran.

—You're kidding—

—Hey, Alders—

—Nice glasses – Somebody lifted them off. Sinclair watched as if they were someone else's, as his glasses were passed from hand to hand.

Suddenly it annoyed him a lot. Suddenly he put up his hand. He looked at it. How had it got there? He couldn't make his mouth work either:

—Pleath, he said, —I *want* to be Edthcumbe like-you-said-I-could.

A hush fell immediately and everyone looked at Parky.

Parky's mouth twitched.

No one said anything at all.

—An' I *will* be Edthcumbe, not All-de-bum, Sinclair demanded.

The challenge in Sinclair's eyes didn't escape Parky's

attention. *So name me after the dead boy – I know what I want, and I'm not afraid, so what?*

—I think you mean Aldebran, Parky said at last. He'd never met anyone like Sinclair. He didn't seem to react like other people. He noted Sinclair's self-reliance; the distance between him and the others; the way Sinclair had plenty to say for himself, when every other monkey he'd ever netted out on the streets and pacified with SHED had been cowed and ready to fall in with anything he said, by this time. Maybe he'd made a mistake. He could always put this one back. Plenty of other monkeys in the trees in the streets of the Animal City.

—And, Sinclair said, though he cared less by now, —I want my glatheth back.

—Of course, Parky said, meltingly. —Radclyffe – young Edgecumbe's glasses.

Radclyffe handed them back.

Sinclair looped them firmly over his ears, bringing Parky back into focus. —And I want to go home now. Iss the China House, on the High Street?

—All in good time. Parky put on a murderous smile. —Meet Edgecumbe Two, everyone.

As bus monkeys in many-coloured uniforms – some green and gold, some red and gold, some spangled with turquoise and silver – gathered around to check him out, pinch him, and otherwise work out how useful or weak he might be, Sinclair watched, as though in a dream, the workings of Parky's face.

—Young Edgecumbe will work the Holden Line –

Radclyffe, the appropriate uniform?

—Check, said Radclyffe. —Sir.

—Holden Line's green and gold, Wolfie whispered to Sinclair.

—Right, said Sinclair. —What is?

—Your uniform. Never mind.

—Japeth – you'll switch to Corinthian Line; Redmond, you'll stay with Edgecumbe on Holden—

Sinclair/Edgecumbe hardly cared anymore. He sat down on his tyre and let things unfold in front of him like a circus film set in a prison. It made a strange scene; the bus monkeys in their spangled liveries, their buttons flashing, some with birds – parrots – on their shoulders; Parky shouting orders like a Hitler, and behind them the massed ranks of three-tier buses brooding like project housing blocks and everyone and everything bathed green under the halogen lights, so that real greens jumped out as browns and reds as blacks and everything took on a house-of-horror look and why was he so *tired* . . .

Sinclair dozed off. When Wolfie nudged him again, Parky was still barking orders in much the same way that as Monahan he'd barked at Aunt Ping over fat-traps and bacteria counts and all the rest of his Food Inspector thing. Sinclair could almost have laughed. He hadn't changed much at all.

—and as always, no talking to Edgecumbe during his three weeks' probationary period. Six-thirty start tomorrow. That's it. End of story.

Sinclair heard the words coming out of Monahan/

Parky's face, but he couldn't be bothered to make the effort to understand what they meant. Monahan wasn't so bad, he supposed. It wasn't his fault he was hunky-and-not-nice. There was something he was supposed to do for him, wasn't there? Rescue him, or something? He couldn't remember why.

—Got any more of that SHED stuff? he somehow asked Wolfie, his tongue so thick in his mouth it came out sounding like *THED thtuff*.

—Later. Wolfie shrugged.

Why would he want to rescue Monahan, when he could simply stay here and chew SHED? He couldn't be bothered rescuing anyone right now.

It wasn't even as if he liked him.

He could've almost laughed if it'd been funny.

Saving Monahan.

Do me a favour.

Not used to deep feelings either way, Sinclair looked at Monahan and knew that he hated him.

His eyes crossed and he fell over backwards.

Always stick by your ship-mates. A promise is a promise to Bob Ames . . .

Sinclair lay on the ground and started to laugh.

Promising to save someone hunky-and-not-nice for the sake of someone not-hunky-and-nice . . . how unreal was that? What about the others? Had he promised to save Kevin Lee as well, with his stupid name of Redmond and his stupid bleached head saying SCUM or SHED or whatever? What about Mr Davey? Wasn't he saved already?

He was still laughing when he finally fell asleep and

they lifted him into the crash bus and laid him out on
a reclining seat and covered him up with his uniform.

Saving . . . Monahan . . . the Food Inspector . . .
he'd sooner save petrol coupons . . .
Monahan . . . Parky . . . whoever he was . . .
he was just an ugly thug.

14

Castor Oil

Mae Ling ran and ran. Anywhere to get away from the monsters – dripping, green-skinned monsters, revolving slowly to eye her . . . in an ordinary-looking warehouse . . . in otherwise kindly New Pork. Horrible, horrible, horrible. And in Veggie World, where nothing killed anything else with eyes, and Exhibition Cows roamed free, but still the Iyamas revolved in the warehouse, no matter how many Votive Sheep Towers there were, or how many Sweepers swept for life-forms. Now she'd seen them, she would *always know they were there.* Horrible, horrible, horri – KVILLE – HARLEM – FORT GEORGE – YORKVILLE – HARLEM – FORT GEORGE – *STOPS BEYOND QUEENS – ALL STOPS BEYOND QUEENS – ALL STOPS BEYOND QU*

An orange and black Balment Line bus swept by, its electronic destination boards wired with peculiar messages. First it said *ALL STOPS BEYOND QUEENS*, but as it bore down on Mae Ling the messages flickered and changed:

LP ME I'M TRAPPED AUNT PING HELP ME

I'M TRAPPED AUNT PING HELP ME I'M TRA

So close to the traffic on the corner of Lions Square and Seventh that the breath of it lifted her hair and plastered it over her face, Mae Ling stopped and stared. That bus – *had it said Aunt Ping*? Aunt Ping was back in the China House, wokking up somebody's takeaway – wasn't she? Had she messed with that stupid microwave? Was it possible Aunt Ping was trapped? If so, where? Somewhere weirder than *this*?

Mae Ling considered the traffic. As well as the constant hold-ups for cows, pigs, pheasants, fleas or whatever else tiny and animal-like wanted to cross the road, there was something else strange about it, too. *There were hardly any cars.* Almost all the traffic was lorries, cabs and buses – those luxury three-tier jobs that seemed to be everywhere. Mae Ling thought she'd hop on one. She'd probably end up on the rank. With luck, she'd see Kevin Lee.

As soon as she thought she'd hop one, a bus pulled up. Its red and gold doors hissed open. Muzak and hot scented air wafted out. *Lions Square*, BusCom announced. *Riding Imperial Line. Your City Centre Service.*

Inside the luxury Topper its bus monkey ran to and fro, pouring coffee, assisting commuters with seat computer terminals, checking swipe cards, fetching scented wipes and courtesy mints, his gold tassels swinging on his suit, his parrot ducking on his neck. He actually had a *goat* on his bus, and there wasn't a thing he could do about it. Mae Ling didn't envy him.

In a city run *by* kids, *for* animals, with hardly any cars on the roads and millions of buses chuffing diesel substitute instead of petrol – filling stations everywhere said *Gas Up with IyamaCo Extra: Clean, Green & Mean* – the feeling should have been good. Instead it was nightmarish. Dripping dead alligator things flashed across her mind. We have to get out of here – Sinclair, Mae Ling thought, where are you?

Lions Square. Your next stop is Forty Camels Street. Please clear the doors, BusCom nagged.

Lions Square – shouldn't that have been *Times* Square? The bus doors hissed shut again, leaving Mae Ling behind. What would she do for money? As the bus slid smoothly into its bus lane, which were all the lanes that there were, Mae Ling glanced up at the gargantuan MediaMax screen that made the giant electronic face of Lions Square:

VIVORS OF DAYTON OHIO WARN OF IYAMA AGGRESSION*SURVIVORS OF DAYTON OHI *many died Tainted, but survivors warned City officials an attack could take place at*

The news was all about some ship that had gone down in the Pacific.

But as she watched it, the news changed:

WARN OF IYAMA AGGRESSION*HELP ME AUNT PING HELP ME AUNT PING HELP ME

Suddenly the face of Aunt Ping filled the giant screen overhead. —Please, Sinclair, it pleaded, —please somebody turn off the wok. Aunt Ping's giant eyes swam with tears. —I'm in a funny place. Please tell your uncle I'm sorry. I'll try to get back before closing time, I – Sinclair, Mae Ling – help me—

—*Aunt Ping!* Brakes screeched and taxi-cabs cannoned into one another – *thud-thud-thud-thud-thud* – as, flinging herself across four lanes of traffic, Mae Ling appealed to the screen with trembling arms:— Aunt Ping! I'm here! Where are you?

But Aunt Ping had faded already, replaced by the basketball scores.

—There she is!

Mae Ling turned to see a boy – the boy selling grass on the Sheep Tower – pointing her out in no uncertain terms to a group of uniformed men.

—There – see – under the screen – I told you she—

But Mae Ling didn't wait to hear any more. Whatever it was about, she didn't need it. Ducking between taxi-cab drivers popping up angrily from their smashed cabs like nasty flowers after rain, re-crossing the corner of Lions and Seventh, she almost ran into a horse.

His rider told her his name straight away.

—This is Adamantine, he said. —Best police horse in the world. He waits. And waits. However long it takes. He never gets side-tracked; never loses patience. We always get our man.

—Did you want something? Mae Ling looked up.

—You, said Mr Niles, who always had extra curry sauce with his chicken. He patted the saddle behind him. —Hop on – *if you can*.

—Don't tell me you're Chief of Police here, Mae Ling laughed. —I know it's you, Mr Niles. I'm sorry your curry's so late.

—Hop on. Mr Niles meant it.

He waited, manoeuvring his horse to block Mae Ling's escape with tiny tweaks of bit and stirrup and knees. Adamantine's nostrils flared. He eyed Mae Ling and stamped. Hop on – *if you can*. It wasn't an invitation; more a command.

A crowd had gathered by now. Mae Ling had been on a horse only one other time in her life. This time would make the second.

—Good boy. She patted the sleek black neck. Adamantine didn't shy.

Setting her foot in the stirrup, she gripped the beautifully-tooled saddle of some kind of alligator skin. Before she could haul herself up, Mr Niles had done it for her. Righting herself in the saddle behind him, Mae Ling found herself a good few metres off the ground, in the middle of a traffic pile-up in Animal City, on the handsomest horse in the world.

—Whaddya think? Mr Niles made Adamantine circle Votive-Sheep-Tower-boy, who had just turned up at a run.

—So it climbs on a horse, so what? That doesn't mean a thing, Sheep-Tower boy sneered. —They can

131

block the way they smell sometimes. Sometimes they even smell *nice*.

—Manty usually knows. Mr Niles patted Adamantine. He turned in the saddle to face Mae Ling, his stomach straining under his uniform. —She don't smell so bad to me.

—It's pretending it's someone called Jessica Dressler. It'll show up at the Station.

—It better. Mr Niles turned Adamantine. —We'll be back for you if you're wrong. You can expect all the tests yourself.

—Test me all you want. Sheep-Tower boy backed off. —I'm not scared of tests.

—Can't trust anyone, can you? Mr Niles narrowed his eyes. —They're getting tricky these days.

—Iyama are always tricky.

Mr Niles considered the Votive vendor.

—So they are, he said.

Putting spurs to Adamantine, Mr Niles took Sixth, then Copperhead; then Elk Street and Roebuck; on to Jackrabbit; finally on to Gopher and Eagle.

On the corner of Eagle and Cougar, —Where are we going? Mae Ling managed to ask between gripping with her knees and holding on with both hands. Adamantine was a white-knuckle ride, all right. But a white-knuckle ride to *where*?

—Precinct Station. Hold on. We got two blocks to go. Mr Niles had got himself an *accent*. Had he forgotten he was Cornish? Mae Ling had got used to his blaring vowels when he ordered.

Incomprehensible to start with, she'd finally understood what he meant by *Aaf-a-rose chicken n' chips an I'll ev they King Prawns in batter with a lod o' that sweeden zour zauce.*

But understanding Cornish wouldn't help her now.

What was it all about?

She found out under the lights of the NPPD Buffalo Precinct Police Station, with Adamantine stabled somewhere beneath its endless dusty corridors, and the horrible dusty coffee more than she could stomach. They fed her, too – a weird mixture of fatty things; pizza, fudge cake, cheese dip, corn-chips, ice-cream – but Mae Ling ate everything she could. She hadn't realised how hungry she was; so what if she ate alone under a video camera in a hollow little room like a toilet attendant's office?

Mr Niles snapped in at the door. —Got everything you want?

He eyed the empty tray of food.

—So now – I have a few questions.

—So do I. Mae Ling wiped her mouth. —What am I here for, for starters? When do I get out? Have you seen Sinclair, my cousin, he's ten with glasses and he looks a bit sad and nerdy—

—One thing at a time, okay?

Mae Ling felt thoroughly cross. Who did Niles think he was?

—Who are you really? she said. —I mean, apart from some old fat guy who always orders curry or chicken?

Niles the Police Chief bridled. —The name's Cherry, he said. —And this is Pitt—

An ugly boy hopped in on one leg.

—Pitt the *Younger*, of course.

—Wasn't he a prime minister or something? Mae Ling raised an eyebrow. He looked a bit like a crow. It was hard to take the ugly boy seriously. He used one leg in a surprised kind of way, as though he'd mislaid the other. His stick rapped a tattoo on the horrible green linoleum as he steadied himself with a bottle. A bottle of *what*, Mae Ling wondered.

—A prime minister? What's that? Ugly boy Pitt drew out a large silver spoon.

—The head of the government, of course – a really important person.

—Not like me, then. Pitt grinned. —I only do this. Raising his spoon, he pretended to swallow something. —And this. He pretended to be sick – Ain't it so, Chief Cherry?

Niles/Cherry nodded. —He's what you might call an expert.

—Guess what my specialty is? Pitt the Younger brought up his spoon suggestively. Whipping off the top of his bottle, he poured out a brimming spoonful of golden liquid, eyeing Mae Ling as he did it. Yes, his eye said, this is for *you*. Pretending to lick the top of the bottle as though it were something delicious, he advanced his brimming spoon.

—Open wide.

—You're joking, right?

Pitt the Younger simpered. —Oh, he said, —if I *were*.

—It's a test, Chief Cherry explained.

—What for?

—Just take it.

—What is it?

—Castor oil.

—But – that'll make me sick. Mae Ling felt sick already.

—You wish. Pitt the Younger grinned.

—You *want* to make me sick?

—How else can we know?

—Know what?

—You're not Iyama.

Mae Ling gave up. The brimming spoon bore down on her. She didn't want – she wasn't *going* – to take it. They seemed to think she was someone else – *it's pretending it's someone called Jessica Dressler*, loathsome Sheep-Tower boy had said – someone not even human. Mae Ling's gorge rose. It wouldn't take much to make her hurl; especially when she remembered the battered Iyama steak she'd eaten in Central Park.

Somewhere underneath all this there was something deeply scary. What could she do to convince them she was human, after all?

—That's it – easy does it – Ugly boy Pitt gripped her nose, his spoon at her lips, his face close to hers, his mouth open in anticipation of the enormous gulp of castor oil she would be forced to swallow next minute.

136

Mae Ling pursed her lips and held her breath. The spoon hovered between them.

—Come on, come on, come on – Pitt wheedled.

—Come on, open wide – He opened wide himself.

Mae Ling made a sudden movement; the spoon swung from her mouth to his; tripping on Pitt's yellow teeth, it flooded his mouth with twenty millilitres of high grade castor oil obtained from seeds of the plant *Ricinus communis*, as Mae Ling read on the label. Pitt the Younger spluttered.

—'Em-et-ic in overdose', Mae Ling read interestedly. —What does emetic mean?

—Mm-m-makes you ill. Pitt swallowed greenly.

—It says here 'Results within minutes.'

— 'Scuse me, Pitt mumbled, —I don't feel so good. Sorry about this Chief Cherry, he said, —I won't let this happ – Turning greener still around the gills, he dashed out holding his mouth.

Mae Ling turned to Police Chief Cherry. By comparison with the obnoxious Pitt he looked like the Christmas tree fairy.

—Isn't there any other test I can take? she asked him, really quite sadly.

Police Chief Cherry nodded.

—Try these lemons, he said.

Later in the office downstairs, at the central computer for Buffalo Precinct, they traced Sinclair Kuet on computer.

—He's been seen on the rank, Officer Aileen

Sweetpea assured them, processing the computer simulation of Sinclair painstakingly built up by Mae Ling. Mae Ling smelled strongly of lemons, having rubbed them all over her skin, this being proof enough, Chief Cherry had assured her, that she wasn't – couldn't be – Iyama. No Iyama could tolerate real lemons, only the made-up kind that they manufactured themselves, which weren't really lemons at all.

—The bus rank? With Kevin/Redmond? Mae Ling listened up.

—BusLink Central. Holden Line. Sweetpea brought up the details.

—Any video? Chief Cherry asked.

—Sure. Sweetpea keyed VID and an image jumped up onscreen.

—*Oh.* Mae Ling cupped her nose. It was – it really was Sinclair. Sinclair caught on security video at the BusLink Depot in a green and gold uniform, talking on the rank with other boys all dressed the same—

—Bus monkeys. Sweetpea zoomed in on them. — What can I tell you?

—only *not* the same, in different colours, and all of them flashed with buttons and badges and epaulettes and turned out like a band-box, and all of them as nerdy as Sinclair, except for one.

—That'll be Brent Wolfram Crossman – Big Wolfie C., they call him.

—We keep an eye on him, Cherry said. —He's coming up to thirteen.

Mae Ling frowned. —So?

—Apprentice Greeters – bus monkeys – have a habit of having accidents before they turn thirteen. That's when they go on the payroll. It's the law.

Like so much in the Animal City, it left a nasty taste in the mouth.

—I have to go to him, Mae Ling said. —Sinclair can't stay there.

Police Chief Cherry nodded. —Those monkeys get a raw deal.

Great. Mae Ling thought bitterly. In a city where *real* monkeys strip shops of food and nobody moves to stop them, my sad nerdy cousin gets exploited in some sinister organisation that makes you into a monkey and dumps you before you're thirteen.

—Penny for 'em.

Police Chief Cherry was watching her.

—I'm thinking – Mae Ling sighed. —Nothing's what it seems to be.

—You think I'm someone else, right?

Mae Ling nodded mutely.

Chief Cherry searched her face. —You have to believe me when I tell you I'm not who you think I am. There's nothing sinister about it. It's just a simple mistake.

Mae Ling returned his gaze. As sure as she saw him in front of her, he was fat Mr Niles who came in the shop for a curry – or the *image* of fat Mr Niles. *Supposing he was a monster himself?* She even found herself sniffing. They smelled of metal, apparently. That was the smell they made.

—Everyone has to trust someone. Chief Cherry understood. —Trust me, you made a mistake.

Would Adamantine have carried a monster around? Maybe in this future world of many future worlds, Chief Cherry looked like Niles, the way she looked like Jessica, whoever Jessica was.

Suddenly Mae Ling smiled.

—Okay, she said. —I trust you.

It seemed such a big thing to say in this city of surprises, this Veggie World, which had seemed so promising to start with, but had a million unexplained edges.

Suddenly Mae Ling felt sick of it all.

—I have to go now, she said.

But another image jumped up in response to an onscreen Search. Officer Sweetpea's fingers worked busily over the keyboard. This time the scene was the Sheep Tower. The grass vendor who'd turned in Mae Ling so sneakily shifted his packets of grass around in his tray and watched the tourists closely. Suddenly he yawned and a long green jaw filled with teeth popped out – and back again, in an instant. *Whaaa–?* Had she seen it? Really? Mae Ling rubbed her eyes.

Chief Cherry was in no doubt. —Send out Adamantine. He can fetch Peter Timmis himself.

—Peter Timmis, sir? The uniformed man by the door came smartly to attention.

—The Votives vendor who paged us earlier. Ride

to the N.C.H. Tower. Manty'll sniff him out. He didn't smell too great at the time. Now I guess he reeks.

The officer turned and went out.

Mae Ling didn't envy him. Poor Sheep-Tower boy. He'd certainly grassed her up, but now the heat was on *him*.

—Look what he brought on himself, she couldn't help saying.

—It happens. Chief Cherry shrugged. —They think if they turn people in, it puts 'em above suspicion. They end up fingering themselves.

—Who?

—Your boyfriend's Iyama, what did you think? They're not so smart, you see.

Sheep-Tower boy was a *monster*? The yawning was weird, okay, but did it have to mean he was a thing like the things inside the warehouse? Mae Ling had trouble imagining it, until Chief Cherry moused IyamaVID.

Onscreen a man on security video crept through darkened stables. As he reached Adamantine, Adamantine stood on his leg. The man thrashed about like a puppet, but Adamantine remained firm. Suddenly the man's leg inflated; puffed up and grew green and spiny; a tail ballooned out behind it; and the man's head disappeared. In his place was a fully-formed monster, thrashing and clashing it's spines and howling in rage and fear.

—One heckuva 'Yama buster. Cherry shook his head admiringly. —Manty decked that feller. Stood on it all night. We peeled it off the floor next morning. He never moved a muscle.

Manty stood on it all night. He never moved a muscle.

Poor Peter Timmis. Imagining Adamantine's determined clop through the marble halls of the Sheep Tower to fetch him back to the Station, Mae Ling almost felt sorry for him – it – whatever it was; the thing that had called her Jessica.

—I'm turning you out on condition you spy. You see anything suspicious, you report to us on this one, okay? Police Chief Cherry rubber-stamped her release.

But Mae Ling hardly heard him. In the city of animals, even monsters deserved a bit of pity – didn't they?

Wasn't it possible, after all, that Iyama were misunderstood?

15

ON THE RANK

His parrot was misbehaving today. Sinclair was pretty teed off with it. He'd smacked it twice on the beak already, fed up with it pecking his cheek. He'd even tapped it once with a biro, but it had thrown the biro down. It wasn't his fault he'd been assigned a stroppy parrot. He had a job to do, the same as it did. He didn't peck *it*, did he?

The parrot's name was H3, for Holden Line, 3 Type: Luxury Topper, which was the name of the bus it was attached to. Aitchthree wasn't any particular picnic to have on your shoulder. For one thing, he pooed on your back, so that Sinclair was forced to change his hygiene bib more frequently than he would have liked to. He would have liked to have rolled H3 up in it and chucked it in the gutter. But that morning, out on the Knoxville run, he had more important things on his mind, like punters on three decks reclining their seats and keeping up a stream of demands. From 'Babywipes please' to 'More coffee', to 'How do I access TV?' Sinclair had more on his plate than he could usefully cope with, *without* a parrot pecking his neck.

—Edgecumbe, can I get a refill?

—Oh, sure. Sinclair/Edgecumbe smiled and poured, the steam from the freshly-brewed coffee curling up and refreshing his face. His uniform that day was crisp and newly-sponged. His gold braid swung on his shoulders as he offered Mrs Neiderstein the cup.

—Will that be all, Mrs Neiderstein?

He knew she didn't take milk or sugar.

—Thanks, Edgecumbe. That'll be fine.

She smiled and tipped him a heavy coin stamped with an Eagle's head.

—See you tomorrow, Edgecumbe.

—Have a nice day, Mrs Neiderstein.

Mrs Neiderstein sat down. A girl in a Street Sweeper's uniform made Sinclair a kiss-my-butt face. She didn't understand. You *had* to brush your uniform and look smart and smile all the time. How else were you going to get tips? Like *she* had a neat job, or something. Sweeping the street for life-forms – how scuzzy was *that*?

Sinclair straightened his gold braid and topped up his coffee machine. He looked cute in his uniform and he knew it. *Cute* meant earning eagle-headed coins and smiling a lot and doing whatever you could all the time and never, ever, wanting to sit down so long as anyone on the decks of your bus ever wanted anything. That was being a bus monkey. And a bus monkey was what he was.

It also meant smelling out Iyama. That was where

144

Aitchthree came in. Iyama-detecting parrots were standard with every bus. Nothing was so sensitive to that sickly metal-based odour; nothing screeched so loud when it smelt it, or smelt it from so far away. Parrots were tops for detecting. Nothing could touch them since canaries had gone down mines to – why *had* they gone down mines?

Sinclair was still wondering why canaries had gone down mines when someone handed in a mouse. Sinclair didn't mind mice. The bus was alive with them, anyway. They regularly bit through wires and shorted computers so that all seat terminals were down when Monday morning came around; but in a bus in the Animal City, no one could turn them out. As well as the onboard mice, the commuters riding downtown to start their day at the office had a collection of animals with them already that Sinclair had learned to cope with. Ferrets up sleeves were popular; snakes were living jewellery; but a big hawk on your arm was cool as *beans*, preferably a kestrel or a merlin.

Sinclair wanted one badly, but meanwhile he kept a bag of chicken heads for customers' hawks, which had been an enormous problem to get hold of, since no one, anywhere, killed chickens. Finally he'd found a dingy shop in an alley. *Clones*, it was called. Underneath the sign which said *Clones*, in very small letters Sinclair read: *Simulated Animals & Animal Parts*. Now he regularly bought 'chicken' heads from the funny little man behind the counter. Sometimes he thought he heard a series of clicks as he entered and left the shop. Once he found a bluish-red spine on the floor, and something dark stirred in his mind; but he broke open a new bar of SHED that night and didn't think any more about it.

With SHED he could cope with anything. He got a regular supply of the chocolate through Redmond, who spent all his wages on SHED and was always happy to share it, whenever he wasn't being bitter and twisted out on the Balment Line, which ran through some pretty heavy areas. Sinclair could only dimly remember having wages. Parky had said they were 'In hand', whatever 'In hand' meant. But with SHED you were always happy, and when you weren't happy, more SHED would fix it. What did he need wages for, when he had his bus to crash in, and the rank buzzed with company by night, and Redmond scored occasional hampers filled with Squeeza-pizza, pretzels, eclairs and Dr Frankie's Horror Jelly Shapes by hacking into company accounts? Except for Aitchthree, the parrot with 'tude, everything was cool and peachy, and everything beyond the rank a little hazy – what more could he possibly want, or had ever wanted?

The Town & Country Line Topper sighed smoothly to a standstill.

This stop Upper Beast Side, BusCom droned. *Please clear the doors. Next stop, Ox Hill East.*

Quickly Sinclair manned his Greeter's cubicle as a tide of commuters washed on, swiping their BusLink account cards past the scanner as they boarded.

—Hello, my name is Edgecumbe and I'm pleased

to serve you today. Welcome to Town & Country Line. Please buzz me if you need anything—

His eyes swept over them expertly. No hawks this morning, he noticed; so much the better for the mice. Even in Animal City, animals ate one another – a disgusting habit, Sinclair thought. One they should try to grow out of.

Please clear the doors, BusCom insisted. *Please clear the doors, please clear the—*

Sinclair leant on the *Doors Open* button as an Exhibition Cow lazily nosed his feet. He mustn't push, or hurry it. He'd got used to animals boarding by themselves. Cats and goats were the worst. He'd even found a hamster in his coffee machine once, nesting in the filters. He'd had to lay it reverently on a wall. *No Excuse for Cruelty to Animals*, the hoardings on Raven Street reminded him.

Sinclair shifted his feet impatiently. Come on, come on, come on. At last the cow backed away, party-poppers from some children's party in Iyamaburger it had gate-crashed some time in the past, swinging from its horns. At last now they could go. Sinclair released *Doors Open*.

They'd very nearly pulled away when the old man tried to board.

Appearing out of nowhere, he flung his stick in the doors and elbowed them open, introducing his hoary old head into the bus ahead of a stringy-looking overcoat. Immediately his head had appeared, the parrot Aitchthree went ballistic:

BWAARK – KER – BWEERKER – WARK – WARK–*WARK!*

The old man took out a swipe card.

WERK – WERK – *WARK!* Aitchthree danced up and down. His crest rose in indignation. Something about the old man. There could be no doubt about it. BRAK-BRAK-BRAK-*BERK!*

—I'll take that. Sinclair took the old man's swipe card. —Jeremiah Burkett, he read.

Then he said, —I don't *think* so, and forced the old man off the bus.

The old man fought like a demon. In the end Sinclair had to place his foot squarely in the small of his stringy old back and shove him out on to the sidewalk. With astonishing strength the old man clawed his way back onto the bus, so that Sinclair was forced to prise him off the inside rail and close the doors on his hands. Even then, he didn't give up. As the bus tried to pull away, he followed it shouting and banging. Then he suddenly disappeared and someone screamed.

Sinclair noticed the small scrap of fabric too late. The old man's coat had been caught in the doors. Opening them as soon as his driver made an emergency stop, Sinclair caught his breath, though he knew what he would find.

Under the wheels of the Luxury Topper lay a sorry mash of squashed limbs and overcoat. The old man's hand clasped and unclasped convulsively, turning, as Sinclair watched it, from veined milky-white to green. A thick tail lashed under the wheels and lay still. The

Iyama's mouth hung open revealing triple rows of yellow teeth, one row inside another. It eyed Sinclair meaningfully, then uncaringly, as the Iyama–breath left its body. Sinclair felt a tug at his heart; then all that was left was a mess in the road that would have to be reported to the authorities.

Surrounded now by his passengers, Sinclair felt tears fill his eyes. They spilled down his face as they gave him a round of applause. Suddenly he was hero of the moment.

—Way to go, Edgecumbe! You showed it!

—See the way it fought back?

—Hey, Champ – three rounds before breakfast!

—Nice going, Edgecumbe – that foot in the back really nailed it!

Edgecumbe tasted a metal taste. He smelled a metal smell.

—I turned it out, he said. —I didn't mean to *kill* it.

—Hey – so what?

—One less Iyama's good news.

—You got that sucker, Edgecumbe.

—Good work, son. Congratulations.

—You should be proud of yourself.

He should be, but he wasn't.

Edgecumbe felt sick to his stomach. He took off his hat and stared at it.

—Shut up, he said. —Shut up. Shut up, shut up, shut *up*.

That night on the rank he was miserable. Not even

SHED picked him up. It simply made him quiet. But it couldn't take the day away. Not even Parky raging around the rank could alter what had happened. Edgecumbe couldn't have cared, that night, if Parky had stripped him of his uniform and turned him out on to the streets. He was always in a foul mood lately. There'd been a bus-boys' strike only a week or two before, and Parky was on a crackdown, so that the only peace they got was when he went home at night, and bus monkeys of every colour and livery gathered to binge on the buses.

—Squeeza-pizza? Redmond offered him a tube of something.

Edgecumbe shook his head.

—You have to eat.

—No, I don't. I don't *have* to do *any*thing.

—I'll tell Mrs Hathurst.

—I'm scared.

Mrs Hathurst was the grim old bat who watched over them. Welfare Officer, that was a joke. Edgecumbe eyed the brooding figure who guarded the rank after hours. Seated high in her office behind banks of security monitors, she knew who did what by night. She even knew Redmond ordered grocery hampers from SuperMart Home Deliveries; what she didn't know was, he charged them to company accounts, for which Parky would have had his *liver*, had he known.

Redmond was clever, hacking into spreadsheets he shouldn't, using weekly company codes. Mrs Hathurst watched her monitors and saw Redmond playing *Dollygun* or some other computer game, on one or other of the seat terminals bus boys were allowed to use by night. She thought he was too SHEDed up to do anything clever. But Redmond, the spit and *image* of Kevin Lee, was more than a match for Mrs Hathurst. There was a limit to how long he was going to get away with it. But until then – Enjoy, Redmond grinned, handing out muffins and Star Bars from a 'Special Occasions' hamper stiff with good stuff.

—Don't mind if I do. Wolfie helped himself. — Who's that, then? he asked, round a cupcake.

The lonely figure under the electronic destination board had bothered Edgecumbe for some time. The way she stood. The cast of her moon-shaped face under hair as smooth as a blackbird's wing. The way he imagined from looking at her – was she? – she might be looking at *him*.

He watched her cross the puddles to stand under Mrs Hathurst's office tower. It was obvious she wanted to reach him. But she didn't want to show herself.

—Friend of yours? asked Wolfie, licking his lips.

Edgecumbe was feeling something. He wasn't sure what it was.

—It's someone I used to know, he said, as Mae Ling stepped out into the light.

He watched as the figure signalled him; signalled back *Okay*, when Mrs Hathurst happened to turn her head; and the figure made its dash to his bus across the wet and ringing depot where the smaller bus monkeys

sobbed with loneliness in corners and no one noticed
or cared – and beyond them New Pork slept uneasily
over sewers alive with alligators, lizards, king python,
rats and coypu. With luck, she'd make it – *yes* – before
Mrs Hathurt saw her coming.

—*Open the doors!* Edgecumbe sat up, electrified.

Somehow she'd passed security hounds B4 and 5;
crossed an electric sensor without triggering the beam;
dodged surveillance cameras from several directions
together. Whoever she was exactly, she'd gate-crashed
the rank by night in the teeth of Hathurst's security
lights and in Mrs Hathurst's face. Cool. She had to be
brave to do *that*.

Redmond opened the doors as the figure flung
itself in. The figure paused; tossed back its hair – and
threw itself on Edgecumbe.

—*Sinclair! I found you!*

—I'm sorry? Edgeumbe backed off. He didn't like
bodily contact, much less with damp people he only
just knew, or only just *thought* he might know.

—Let me look at you. The girl with the blackbird-
wing hair considered his uniform, half-undone now,
but still blazed with Town & Country Line tassels in
white and deepest maroon. —Wow, she said. —What
are you *like*?

—I don't know. What *am* I like?

Edgecumbe looked into her face and something
stirred in his mind. The whiff of cooking bean sprouts;
someone shouting orders through a cheesy plastic
strip-curtain – *two egg-fried rice, sweet and sour pork,*

three pancake rolls and two banana fritters – Sinclair, have you got that?

—Cool bus – are they all like this?

—Haven't you been inside one? Edgecumbe was incredulous. Who hadn't caught a Topper?

—Anyway. I made it. Mae Ling flopped into a seat.

—So this is where you live.

—Some of the time.

—*Most* of the time. Wolfie joined them curiously.

Screening her from Hathurst's camera with his jacket, which would give them about ten minutes before she noticed and came screeching over to see what the trouble with it was, Redmond looked from the girl to Edgecumbe, from Edgecumbe back to the girl.

—So – you know each other?

—No. Yes. Edgecumbe felt really mixed up. —Sort of. Some of the time.

His cousin Mae Ling lay dripping wet on deck two of Edgecumbe's Town & Country Line Topper, with half-a-dozen Imperials and Corinthians gaping at her over a half empty grocery hamper, and *still* he searched for her name.

—How did you know I was here? was the best he could do.

—I saw you on computer, you dope. Mae Ling leaned forward seriously. —We have to get out of here. *Now*.

Edgecumbe thought she looked needlessly worried.

—Here, he said, —have some SHED.

—Have you seen Aunt Ping? I think she's trapped somewhere.

This was another poser that made the cogs in Edgecumbe's brain spin around. He broke off some more SHED himself. —Hello, he said, —my name is Edgecumbe, and I'll be serving you today—

—Stop eating that stupid chocolate and listen to me. Mae Ling brought out some lemons and wafted them under his nose. —We're trapped here, I don't know how, but we've got to get back. Something horrible's going to happen, I don't know what—

—Don't know much, do you? Redmond said.

—Welcome to Town & Country Line – Edgecumbe droned. —Please clear the doors. Thank you.

—You're Tainted, Mae Ling said sadly. —Get me some liquid. Anything.

—This do? Wolfie cracked open a Ritalin Extra.

Drinking the top off and squeezing in a couple of lemons, which she had in a bag cut in halves, Mae Ling turned it over to Edgecumbe.

—Drink and listen. You're Sinclair Kuet, not Edgecumbe. You come from the China House Takeaway and you're pretty hot with orders, but you *can* lose your temper sometimes when things don't turn out right.

His head cleared as Edgecumbe gulped.

—Robert Ames gave me these – what are they called?

—Lemons. Mae Ling rubbed some over him.

—But I dropped them and ran – and Robert Ames
– and Bob Ames, he got burned.

—Yes, Mae Ling said, —it's horrible here—

—Depends on the way you look at it, Redmond
put in.

—Your name is Sinclair, not Edgecumbe—

—My name is Sinclair. Hello.

Mae Ling turned on Redmond. —And *your* name
is Kevin Lee.

—No way.

—How long have you been here, then?

—I don't remember, exactly. Redmond scratched
his head.

—Your haircut – did it say SCUM once?

—No, it always said SHED.

—You're sure about that?

—No.

—I *am* Sinclair, Sinclair remembered. —And I'm
Tainted because I – spent too long with Iyama on a
boat, and I'm stupid because of S-SHED, and you –
he regarded the girl with the blackbird-wing hair –
and you, you're my *cousin*, Mae Ling!

—So how did you get here? Mae Ling repeated,
really wanting to know.

—We went in a mist, Sinclair remembered, —and I
didn't know where I was.

—What mist?

—On the *Annaho*. It made everything go funny, and
there were these pilots, like: 'Help me, boy! Come
back!'—like I'm *going* to stay in 1942 with them or

something, just because we got stuck in a 'nomaly—

—A what?

—A place where normal rules don't apply, Sinclair explained happily.

Mae Ling looked at her cousin, wondering if normal rules had *ever* applied.

—I mean before all that, she said testily. —How did you get here to start with?

Sinclair thought deeply.

—That would be the microwave.

—Exactly, Mae Ling agreed.

—Hathurst Alert. Wolfie checked the office window. —I'd say you've got two minutes before she blows.

—And it was weird – Sinclair gabbled.

—What was?

—After the pilots, and everything – I saw Aunt Ping – in a rose—

—Aunt Ping in a *rose*?

—And Dimmie Sum. And—

—Yes?

—She was waving and—

—What?

—It was like, Iyama *World*. Iyama were everywhere.

Mae Ling seized Sinclair's arm. —We've got to get out of here now.

—*One* minute, Wolfie warned.

—It's horrible here. They *eat* Iyama. There's going to be a war.

—No. Sinclair said, —it isn't like that.

She hadn't time to convince him.

—Yes, Mae Ling said, —it *is*.

—Mrs Hathurst says you can't believe everything you see on the news.

—Who's Mrs Hathurst?

—Our Welfare Officer—

—Your *Welfare* Officer—

—She gives us SHED—

—I bet she does—

—She's coming over now.

Unable to sort out his feelings, Sinclair rocked to and fro as Mrs Hathurst bore down on them under a full head of steam.

—*Operatives Edgecumbe and Wolfram! If I find interference with surveillance cameras you'll work three extra shifts!*

Sinclair swallowed. Mrs Hathurst could be exceptionally nasty. She had a gift that way. The thought jumped in Sinclair's brain – why not go before she reached them? *He had to rescue everyone, Kevin Lee included.* Mae Ling was right. This was a horrible World. He had to do it *now*.

—*Redmond, I hope that's not you. You know what'll happen, don't you?*

Mrs Hathurst stormed across the puddles. The only thing holding her up was the enormity of her rage.

Redmond moaned. —She'll do me. She did me the other day.

—I calculate we have an eighty-four per cent chance of escaping if we unlock the security codes. Sinclair turned to Redmond. —Can we unlock the security codes and open the driver's cab?

Hope leapt in Redmond's face as he suddenly saw that they could.

—Consider it done.

Turning to the program he had open already on a nearby seat terminal, he rapidly keyed in passwords he felt he'd known since birth.

Everyone bolted who was going to, Corinthians and Balment Line monkeys scuttling rapidly off the bus with their parrots bobbing on their shoulders, before the Hathurst was close enough to register names or faces. Rats off a sinking ship, Sinclair thought, suddenly remembering the *Annaho* and the bravery of the company in the hold. Good riddance to gutless wonders.

Only Redmond and Wolfie remained.

—Take me with you, Wolfie begged. —I'll be thirteen next week – you know?

Sinclair nodded, remembering the fate of Edgecumbe One and how many other rising thirteens the company hadn't wanted to register or officially put on the payroll. Wolfie would be lucky to see the inside of next week before a bus backed over him in the depot, and another unfortunate accident was entered in company records.

—We want you to come, he said simply.

Wolfie snapped the doors shut under the Hathurst's nose. Sinclair vaulted over him to throw himself at the driver's cab, which magically opened as Redmond overrode its security program with one swift keystroke, moving rapidly on to disable the Stationary Alarm and allow Sinclair behind the wheel. Redmond was enjoying himself now. With a shudder that ran through the bus the engine burst into life as he overrode six separate cutouts.

Sinclair put his foot down and the brakes hissed off with a sigh.

—She's going to get in the way! Mae Ling screamed excitedly. —Sinclair – be careful! Look out!

The halogen lights threw down their green pall and showed him Mrs Hathurst, braced in front of the gate.

She meant to block their path the only way she could.

Sinclair swallowed. The only thing that stood in the way of freedom, rescue, escape – was Mrs Hathurst's horrible bulky body. The night stretched away beyond the gate. Was it worth a life?

—STOP NOW! she bellowed bullishly. —*Operatives Edgecumbe and Redmond! STOP AT ONCE, I SAY!*

Sinclair put his foot down and the bus jumped to meet her.

—What are you doing?

—She'll move.

—And if she doesn't?

—Sinclair – no! You can't! Mae Ling's voice rose on a scream.

But Sinclair found that he could. This was war – the second time, that day, he would strike a blow without meaning to.

Revving the lovely smooth engine of the Luxury Topper, Sinclair felt it automatically engage third gear as he smashed through the gates and out into the Animal City. Her body hardly stopped the six cylinder engine at all.

Enjoying the feel of its power—

—*No! Sinclair! Don't!*

– he ran Mrs Hathurst down.

16

THE RAMP

—But you couldn't be *sure*, Mae Ling said.

—I saw it yawn the other day, and those teeth – but no, Sinclair said. —I couldn't.

—Is it gone yet?

—Not quite – there it is!

Sinclair peered into his mirror, relieved.

—Did you see it jump out of the way? Mae Ling joined him in his security-sealed cab, usually the home of his driver, Usborne, who hardly ever spoke and was surly whenever he did, in the way of drivers sealed in for hours who have grown to love their own company. Sinclair pictured his face. He would be even more surly next morning, with no bus to be surly in.

—I thought I hit it, he said.

Mae Ling's face was pale.

—It, like, rolled and jumped at the very last minute. Tough as nails, aren't they?

Sinclair was glad that it was.

Instead of being the second of its kind smashed on the streets that day, the Iyama-that-had-been-Hathurst clung grinning to the gates behind them in its shreds of Hathurst clothing, lashing its tail with rage. So it had been a gamble. So he was glad that he'd won.

—Was *that* Hathurst? Redmond looked back at it, astonished.

—Looks like it, Sinclair said.

—You mean – *she's always been Iyama*? Wolfie's jaw dropped.

—Looks like it, Sinclair said.

—But how could it work on the rank so long? Redmond wondered aloud, the scales suddenly falling from his eyes. —How could it work with the *parrots*?

—It never did, Sinclair reminded him. —Parky dealt with the birds.

How could they not have put two and two together before and come up with a Big Green, he wondered. What were they, deaf and blind?

—But still? Redmond tried to work it out.

—I don't know, Sinclair said. —They're clever.

—No, they're not, Mae Ling said with certainty. — They're not clever at all, just desperate.

—Why are they desperate?

—We attack them all the time – wouldn't *you* be? 'People were scared of Iyama, and when people get scared all sorts of good things like friendship and trust and the rest of it, well, they go to the dogs.' That's what Robert Ames told me.

Sinclair swallowed. A cold breath of mist seemed to touch him. Who was the monster, here? He'd only gambled on running, or not running, something down

– and that was all right, just because it wasn't *human*? He liked himself better as Edgecumbe, who'd thrown down his hat in distress and regretted the mess in the road.

—I wonder how many there are, Mae Ling whispered, as the Animal City fell behind them.

—Out of the people I've met so far, about half have been Iyama. Sinclair remembered the battling hordes of the *Ulan Bator*. —That makes it one in two.

—One in two – it *can't* be. Mae Ling cupped her face in her hands. —It's not all their fault, she said.

The wailing alarms of the rank faded far behind them. Sinclair swung out on the Beasthaven Bridge, the river gleaming beneath him like a snake.

—Where to? he asked.

—Out of town. Somewhere out of this horrible place, Mae Ling said wildly as the bridge arches peeled away in front of her – *thrum-thrum-thrum* – and slipped away past the windscreen.

—It's not *all* bad, Sinclair said, through the afterglow of SHED.

—It *is*, Mae Ling insisted, suddenly remembering the outlines of grim factory sheds against the sky. How could she convince him?

—Get anywhere out of this city, she said. —Follow the signs for Queens.

Queen bees, he supposed. Sinclair followed the signs; over the bridge, necklaced with lights; under the interchange; and onto the freeway on I-84. In no time the city slipped away and the night-wilds of sudden little towns glimmered beneath them; scrub and bushes loomed and disappeared; strange dark outlines of rocks and buildings jumped up and fell away, rose and fell away, as giant container trucks hauled their night-load beside them and Redmond and Wolfie snored – and still the freeway carried them on into the mysterious darkness of a world like, but not like, their own; real, but not-real, nice, but not-nice; Iyama, but not-Iyama.

—Look! Mae Ling pointed. —Follow that truck!

—Where? Sinclair squinted. —You're kidding.

Mae Ling wished that she was. The whiff of the lorry in front of them carried her back to that New Pork backstreet where she'd glimpsed the carnage in the warehouse; those carcasses grinning on their butchers' hooks, revolving slowly to eye her. *Leg joints . . . liver . . . brisket . . . tail . . .*

—Primrose Meadows. Mae Ling could discern the lettering now. Your First Stop for Fresh Iyama.

Sinclair pulled in behind it. —What does that mean? he said.

—It means we follow it. Then I'll show you.

—Show me what?

—Why there's going to be a war?

—There isn't.

—There's going to be *something*.

Mae Ling was right. He opened his mouth, then closed it. For a moment, he felt like panicking.

—I want to go home.

—And I don't?

Sinclair felt a cold hand on his heart. *Run, it's the end of the world.*

—I'm supposed to rescue you all, he said. —You and Kev and David, I mean Napes, and I don't even know where he *is*—

—It's everyone, isn't it? Mae Ling regarded him steadily. —*Everyone in the takeaway that night,* when the microwave—

—Banged in the corner? Sinclair avoided a woodchuck caught in the glare of his lights. —And, he said, Mae Ling—

—Yes?

It took a lot to say it.

—I'm really glad you found me.

—I know. Mae Ling said. —I know.

—I'm Kevin Lee, I'm Kevin Lee, Sang Redmond.

—And Parky is Mr Monahan.

—You're kidding.

—Do I *look* like I'm kidding?

—So we have to take him with us?

—Ultimately, yes.

—What's with ultimately? When do we go?

—Soon as we find a *way* to go, all right? Sinclair turned the engine off, tiring of Redmond's persistence. Kevin *Lee's* persistence.

The Town & Country Line Topper died quietly on the edge of a razor-wired estate. Some minutes earlier, the truck saying 'Primrose Meadows' had winked away in the trees.

—What is it? Why are we stopping? Wolfie smelled of sleep.

—We're at some kind of farm. Mae Ling looked at him crossly. Why had they brought this lump?

—I'm going back to sleep. Wolfie yawned. —Wake me next century, will you?

Redmond had turned over, too. Sinclair looked at Mae Ling. Outside wild things stirred. Branches knocked together in an uneasy prairie wind.

—What do you want to do?

There wasn't much doubt in her eyes.

Mae Ling nodded. —Come on.

They slipped out together into the darkness. Beyond them a metal industrial unit hummed busily in the trees. It went on and on. Like the side of *Titanic*, Mae Ling thought, remembering the factory-farm profile she'd viewed from the top of the Sheep Tower.

There seemed to be no way around it. Inside it something fought with terrible ferocity, snarling and thumping the walls as though to bring down the house. Mae Ling and Sinclair ducked as a uniformed Primrose Meadows guard patrolled the unit, clapping the metal sides as he went along with a nasty-looking baton.

—Shut it, he growled. —Settle down in there, or I'll give you something to settle with.

They waited until the sound of his baton rang deep and distant in the trees. How many units were there? Then Sinclair spotted a racoon, its bandit-like black and white markings flashing under the moon.

—Through here. Sinclair held up the wire where the racoon had led the way.

Mae Ling scrambled under it. Nothing separated them now from the entrance to the massively-humming unit except a million security lights.

—Follow him. Sinclair said, on a sudden inspiration.
—Look, he knows where he's going.

Do I have to spell it out for you? The racoon's black-and-white bandit mask looked back at them as if to say, *What are you, chicken? Come on.*

—He knows the way inside. Mae Ling started up.
—What are we waiting for?

It turned out they were waiting for a heart and a brain. That was all they were missing, as members of the human race. The monsters who had made Primrose Meadows had designed their farm very well.

Production values were charted in detail on the wall:

'This Week's Target: Meat Per Tonne of Feed – 1,897 Kilos

LAST MONTH'S TOTAL! —7,500 kilos produced for less than 2.5 tonnes of feed!!'

What do they feed them *on*? Mae Ling wondered, viewing the seething floor of pens chock-a-block with Iyama. The smell was overwhelming; as soon as they ducked through the dung-covered flap that the racoon had flickered through, Mae Ling covered her mouth. Under the searching arc-lights, motes of dust and rubbish made the atmosphere thick and unbreathable as not-very-functional filters coughed back the recycled air, laden with virus and metal-smell, back at the penned Big Greens.

—It's so hot here. How can they stand it? Sinclair breathed in the sickly air and thought he'd suffocate.

—They don't have a lot of choice. Mae Ling took in the scene and knew they must stick to the wall where internal cameras might miss them. There wasn't much else they might miss; as far as the eye could see pens stretched in every direction, some of them tiered in racks from which bloody red eyes glared down. Iyama maddened by heat and confinement lashed their tails and fought. Some chewed the spines off others for something to do. Others lay there and let them. None of them bothered being human – what was the point?

—It's horrible, Sinclair said. —Isn't it?

—Of course it is. Mae Ling felt faint. —Can you *blame* them for fighting back?

—Why can't they break out? Sinclair wondered.

Mae Ling looked doubtful. —The cages are incredibly strong.

The racoon which had led them in hurried busily past, making for the dung-flap, its mouth distended by a purple-veined egg so huge it could barely carry it.

—Iyama *eggs*? Mae Ling didn't even want to think about it. She didn't want to visualise their horrible captive life-cycle, the – presumably – baby Iyama, presumably born in the unit and crying far into the night under arc-lamps instead of mothers.

—Can we go now? Sinclair said. —I'm going to be sick in a minute.

Aware of a rumbling sound that seemed to fill the building, the earth, the air, Mae Ling looked around for escape. The rumble grew louder; nearer; the very walls seemed to shake. All at once a hopper opened above them and showered the cages with pellets. Iyama threw back their multiple-teethed mouths and fought for a place in the shower, the weakest raving around in the leavings, too sickly to care what they ate. Amongst the press of legs, bodies could clearly be seen. Mae Ling covered her mouth.

—Hurry, she said. —Let's get out.

There wasn't much to stay for. Mae Ling cast a final compassionate eye over the feeding floor and knew things were as bad as they could be. So strange-looking aliens might not have set out out from Iyama World in expectation of love and peace. They might not have the best habits. But surely they deserved more than this. Her eye caught the roving hopper. Under a picture of a grinning Big Green a sign on it read: 'Photon Agricultural Concentrated Protein Feed – 90% Recycled Iyama for Maximum Productivity.'

It seemed like the final straw – the final twist of the knife. *They feed them bits of themselves*, she thought. *They're eating Iyama, mashed up*. She hardly felt the bat of the closing dung-flap as they raced for the gap in the fence; hardly heard Sinclair's anxious plea of Can-you-please-hurry-up; hardly felt the blanket around her body as he tucked her up safe on the bus.

She lay wide-eyed and awake for hours. They had to swallow everything, and there wasn't a thing they could do. They *couldn't even be sick and vomit up bits of themselves*. How much worse, Mae Ling wondered, as she finally fell into a sickly sleep, could one species treat another?

Quite a bit worse, as it happened. The morning dawned bright and red in the east over the city.

Wolfie got up and smelled it. It had an unpleasant feel.

—Smells funny today, he noticed.

—That'll be the farm. Sinclair screwed up his nose.

—Maybe the heat's up too much in the bus. Redmond turned it down.

—No, the weather's funny. Sinclair smelled the east.

—Maybe there's thunder in the air. *Or something else*, he thought.

Redmond heated old pretzels in the mike in the Greeter's cubicle. But Sinclair couldn't eat a thing.

—I'm not hungry, he said. —Where's Mae Ling?

He searched the bus for her wildly. He'd tucked her up last night and made her safe and quiet.

But now her blankets were empty.

—She isn't here, he said. —What's that noise – that whistling? It sounds like—

—What? Wolfie eyed him.

Like the end of the world, Sinclair thought.

—She's probably down at the farm, he said. I'm going out to find her.

Mae Ling wasn't in the bus because she was down at the stunning ramp with the sanitary engineer. So was Mr Skinner-Dreyfus, manager of Primrose Meadows. Skinner-Dreyfus was narrow-bodied, smug, and in possession of all the facts and figures. A half-a-head taller than Marchmant, the sanitary engineer, he wasn't much older than Mae Ling herself, she realised in studying him. Marchmant couldn't have been more than thirteen. Thirteen-going-on-forty. Under their bright yellow hard-hats they might have been men instead of boys; human instead of sub-human.

—How many head through this month? Marchmant asked.

—Fourteen hundred and seventy-two, Skinner-Dreyfus supplied crisply. —Plus a hundred and thirty-four losses.

A hundred and thirty-four losses. *That meant deaths.* Palming a tiny PC, Marchmant tapped in the figures.

The noise was incredible that morning. They had, Skinner-Dreyfus explained, just separated out the young, before the Greenbacks were fully awake, on another part of the farm. The bellowing and whistling continued as he explained. One voice, in particular, stood out:

—EEE-*YOAR-OH! EEEE-YOAR-OH-AAAH!*

—That's one unhappy 'Yama, Skinner-Dreyfus explained. —She wants her babies, all right. She'll forget for a while, then start again. It's like grieving, mourning – people don't know. They don't like to think they have feelings.

—*Sinclair!* Mae Ling made room for him in the brush where she'd hidden herself.

—Stop them making that noise. Sinclair held his head. —It's horrible. I don't like it.

—No one likes it. Mae Ling put her finger to her lips. —Be quiet. I want to see what that thing is.

—How's the new design holding up? Marchmant asked at that moment, eyeing the concrete walkway Mae Ling had had her eyes on.

—The stairway to heaven? Skinner-Dreyfus grinned. —They go up it like lambs and and come down it like bacon. We don't have any trouble.

—He means that ramp, Mae Ling whispered.

—What ramp? Sinclair looked at it and understood. He didn't have to be told what it was for. Its complex design was as clear to him as one of his drawings. A hideous smell wafted down between the gently-sloping walls of the concrete walkway which made two hairpin bends before disappearing at its highest point into a sinister-looking unit. It had everything to do with killing, but if you came from Iyama World, how would you know about that?

—They go up there, see? he pointed up the ramp. —They can't see what's coming because of the bends, so they aren't too stressed out – Sinclair shuddered, feeling it – and they probably have a tendency to go where a leader takes them. So they go up one by one, and then, when they reach the top – Sinclair moved to take a look – probably something kills them.

—Stunners in good order, Mr Skinner-Dreyfus?

the hard-hatted Marchmant was saying.

—A1, said Skinner-Dreyfus, reminding Sinclair of Robert Ames, who used the expression at times. — Funny weather today, Mr Marchmant. Quite a fire in the east, wouldn't you say?

Marchmant looked east at the City and blanched. Never in all his early-morning spot-checks on health and safety at work had he seen a sky quite like it.

—Holy Moses. Marchmant flipped on his car radio. The report that flickered out on the minute was anything but reassuring:

. . . CityNews Special, we are under attack, repeat under attack, repeat clear and present danger. Please stay calm. Stay in your homes. Stay away from anything electrical. Please do not evacuate over Beasthaven Bridge. Please do not board City buses. Please do not block the streets. Do not enter the City. Do not leave the City. CityNews Special, we are under attack, repeat, under attack—

—Looks like trouble on a stick. Marchmant wiped his mouth as the Maser-lights danced over the city.— And then some trouble over.

As the war-cries and bellows of the farm-bound Iyama mingled on the air with the distant smell of burning, Sinclair held his breath as though he might hold the world together, so long as he never let it out. At last he exhaled and his breath streamed out and he knew that this world was the same as any other, and he could never control or understand it.

Something struggled inside him. Then a name burst out.

—Alma!

—Alma? Mae Ling frowned.

—I have to meet her!

—Not back *there*—

—I should have met her before—

—In the City? We *can't*.

But Sinclair had made up his mind. *Run, it's the end of the world*. He felt the pain of the Iyama hot in his veins. It wasn't animals or aliens he minded. It was people he would never understand.

EEE-YOAR-OH! EEEE-YOAR-OH!

—Come on, he said. —Back to the bus. We're not leaving *them* behind.

17

LIONS SQUARE

And they didn't leave many behind them when they drove the maroon-and-white Town & Country Line Topper through the gates of Primrose Meadows Iyama Farm and tore off the ends of Units B4 and B5, releasing the blinking Greenbacks into the stiff dawn breeze that brought them the scent of battle.

—*Woo-hoo! We did it!* Sinclair hooted for all of them as they swung out onto the Interstate trailing Primrose Meadows security fencing ripped clean from its underground supports from both rear fenders behind them.

—You're not wrong! Redmond was enjoying himself now. —See how those monkeys jumped?

He meant Skinner-Dreyfus and Marchmant, who had leapt like scalded cats when the Topper had made its crazed appearance and crashed the gates, deliberately tearing a swathe through the finest commercial producer of Iyama steak this side of Christmas. It was a great rescue, remembered forever after in Iyama lore. The sense of it went down in Iyama legend something like this:

'*The days were dark and* aradnha! *(vile, or something very like it) when* Jalignah *came. Many had come, and all were captured. Many were born in the Primrose. And the Primrose was death to many. And out of that darkness* Jalignah *came, on the day of The Last of Battles. And he let in the light with his mighty* beerst *(vehicle of some kind) and the light streamed down on the many. And the many triumphed over the* wentaleshmel *(humans; literally, bad-smelling-when-near-them) that day. And* Jalignah *reigned forever in The Rose.*'

—Look at them! Mae Ling looked back. —They don't even know how to *walk* they've been caged so long!

Sinclair checked his mirror. It was a truly pathetic sight. Behind them the newly-released horde of Iyama staggered into the sunshine. A few mounted Marchmant's car. Instantly lost under swarming Iyama, in moments its lights were smashed. The vehicle was being rocked to and fro. Marchmant could thank his lucky stars they were taking it out on his car and not on his unlucky hide. Like some dinosaur raising its head from the swamp, the leading Iyama threw back its head and roared on the corpse of the car. Another called; then another; then finally the whole host took up the call.

EEE-YOAR-OH! EEE-YOAR-*A* -*OH-A*!

—That's a new one, Sinclair said. —They don't usually do that last bit.

—What's it mean? Wolfie asked.

—It's a war-cry, Sinclair said.

176

—Great, Wolfie said. —They're frying the City, and we have to let them out *now*?

—How do you know they're frying the City?

Wolfie turned to look at him. —How more obvious can it be?

It was pretty obvious, riding in, as the Maser-bolts played on the towers overhead and brought rubble down from the sky. Packs of running animals streamed away from the City. Other animals streamed in the general confusion. The Town & Country Line Topper careered on through the melée, strange scenes glimpsed then forgotten, strangled shouts of warning clearing their road.

Road-blocks tried to stop them, but Sinclair crashed though them all. People and animals filled the streets in confusion. Mae Ling glimpsed Police Chief Cherry on Adamantine trying to turn back the tide.

—Go back to your homes! he roared. —Stay inside! Don't panic!

Adamantine stamped his perfect black feet, but no one paid any attention. Not even the most adamant horse in the world would turn back the bolts of amplified microwave radiation shafting out from guerrilla bands of Greenbacks storming up from the docks, from the parks, from the very sewers underground, their triple rows of teeth clacking together as they ran, their gleaming spines clashing on their tails.

Over the City hovered the central magnetron in a cloud of mysterious gases, its spinning coils crackling with mischief. To recharge their Masers the Iyama horde had only to hold up their arms, and the amplified microwaves would light them up like Christmas trees and crackle down into their barrels. Somehow immune to burning and nervous system damage, the Greenback army had all the cards in its claws. How would it play them that day? Would it grant any quarter? Had it known any?

Animal City was in a tailspin, anyone could see. A stampede of police horses along Broadway made a temporary road for the massed bears of Central Park to follow through. Goats maddened by rushing people tried to butt out, but no one would make way and let them. Pigs screamed in alleyways; cocks crowed from pediments; and everywhere terrified pigeons streamed black-and-white droppings over crowds too terrified to care.

The smell of singeing was in the air, and everywhere rumour ran rife:

—They got the Bridge—

—No, Newlyn Breaks—

—They got the Breaks already—

—They torched Queens, see the smoke over Queens?

—Stay out of the subway—

—The subway's OK—

—Stay outta the Village, you mean—

—The Village is safe, try the Heights—

—The Heights? You got to be kidding—

Not all places were the same. For some reason

Lions Square made the centre of a pocket of calm. The Village was almost untouched, as well, as the Maser-bolts played on Hen-Battery Park on the southernmost toe of the Island.

Sinclair parked the bus and leapt out. Lions Square! Where he should have met Alma a *week* ago – was it more? If anything was ever late in the day, this was the day it was latest.

Lions Square had changed since Sinclair's Town & Country Line route had last taken him routinely through it. He'd never noticed the Ranter before. He hadn't known Ranters were allowed to set up their soap box in the middle of a sea of traffic. But the end of the world made, he supposed, an exception for road rules enforcement.

—*The end of the world is nigh*, the Ranter ranted, the electric air buzzing around him. —*Let those who will be saved, be saved*—

—*What shall we do?* The crowd pressed him, as the Trade Center hummed with lightning strikes from a suddenly lowering sky. —*Tell us, what shall we do?* The Ranter held up a mouse. —*Let those who strike the least of these beware*—

Behind him the giant television screen which made the electronic eye of Lions Square milled with confused images, one overlapping another. A fisher fishing; a titanic sea; paddy fields under rice; a building falling; margarine spreading; a mantis devouring a beetle; icebergs melting; lions yawning; a car crash; a wedding; a party – all the scenes in a confused world, on and on and on, until Sinclair thought his brain would burst if he watched it another moment. Yet he couldn't look away. The Ranter waved his arms and shouted about Judgement Day and no one could take their eyes off him, as though he might at any moment reveal a code to save the world, because he understood that they were bad, and had brought this upon themselves. And in the moment that he acknowledged the Ranter's power over him – over everyone gathered in Lions Square while the Animal City burned around them – Sinclair saw that the Ranter was *Mr Davey* – or Abel Blamey, as he called himself now; and next to him was Alma; and next to, and around her, the company of the *Dayton Ohio*.

Sinclair's heart leapt. —*Alma!*

He fought the crowd to reach her, but the crowd lifted him up and swept him another way entirely. But suddenly Alma saw him.

—*Sinclair!* He saw her mouth framing his name as on the screen behind her a bull charged a matador, the stockmarket crashed, and a million died in an earthquake.

—*Sinclair – I'm coming – wait—*

He saw her wade into the crowd bringing Abel Blamey, still ranting and raving, behind her.

That was the last thing he saw before Napes reared up in his face.

—Sorry, shipmate. Napes winked.

—Sorry, for what? Sinclair gaped.

—I got secret orders, me.

Inside Napes' mouth its Iyama-tongue flickered over its teeth. It hadn't bothered hiding them. Its spines clicked on its neck, and its bluish-red spinal extensions were fully erect through its clothing, which hung down around it in strings. Still it had retained its Napes' face. Sinclair wondered why it had bothered. Probably just to mix with the crowd, although no one would have noticed if it had rode in screaming on a chariot, so thick was the panic in Lions Square, so loud the plea to *Save us*!

Napes smelled the panic. It would have smiled if it could.

—Game's up, *wentaleshmel*—

—Get off me, will you—

—No tricks, mind. Come along with me.

—Let me go – I hate you—

—Come on now, fishee, fishee—

Napes looked down on its fishee once more, the fishee it had hooked on the *Annaho* and battened down in the hold. This time it's orders were no less pressing. They came from the highest place possible, within certain scent of Planet Rose, home world to every Iyama, and from the mind of The Big Green itself.

The Iyama Napes felt almost sorry for its fishee, and for all fishees like it. But not quite sorry enough.

Lifting its arm with its tattered shirt, it cracked a yawn over Sinclair that showed its teeth to the back of its throat.

EEE-YOAR-OH!

Then it brought down its club on the back of his head and flung him over its back like a rabbit.

18

THE BIG GREEN

—*Jalignah!* The Big Green somehow conveyed, though its mouth had never made words. *You come to save us all!*

—No, Sinclair insisted, —you've got it all wrong. I'm here to save all of *us*. We come from the China House. And now we're going back there, thank you very much.

He didn't care for the smell of the Grand Iyama. The Big Green smelled like he never washed and had just come up from a metal-mine filled with cabbage. Extending its webbed foot quite delicately on the glittering steps of its throne, the King Over All Iyama considered its guest, the war waged beneath them, the reasons for the war waged beneath them, and its troublesome digestive tract. Taking a fruit the shape of a frisbee from a dish overflowing with jewels, it methodically ate its way through it before considering any reply.

—*Jalignah* wears many disguises, it finally decided.

—I told you before, it's nothing to *do* with me. Sinclair felt a tantrum threatening. —And Jaligger isn't my name.

—What *Jalignah* says today, the world must—

—LEAVE ME ALONE! Sinclair shouted.

Napes tapped its club in the corner. It wasn't often allowed on an Imperial Transport Float. Except for its secret mission to catch any agents, it wouldn't be here now. Turned out it had netted *Jalignah* himself. How was it to know? Beneath Napes' webbed feet the battle for the Animal City raged under the transparent floor of the hovering Transporter in the strange space made for the meeting, which in one sense occurred in a speck in the top right-hand-corner of the MediaMax screen on Lions Square, but in some other sense in the sky over the Last of Battles.

King Iyama spread its feet. —*Jalignah* must listen, it said as Superman, then as Lawrence of Arabia. —We have come far. Many have been killed. This is not *our* wish.

Beneath Lawrence of Arabia the war machine hummed. The giant Magnetron spinning its coils over the Snake River was the largest in Iyama World, or in any other. Considerable energy had been taken up in bringing the giant Magnetron through a doorway. It had only been done as a last resort, since doorways were breached anyhow, in a way no Iyama yet understood, but had to do with – *Jalignah*.

Rapidly taking on a succession of other famous faces it had picked up off the History Channel in an effort to make Sinclair as comfortable as it could, the Big Green made its case:

—Doorways *to* and *from* the Rose are of paramount

importance, it said as Abraham Lincoln.

—Are what of what? Sinclair screwed up his face.

—*Jalignah* will understand when I tell him what has happened since first the doorways were opened, the Big Green went on, though it looked like Marilyn Monroe. —The first miners came through in 1947, but prospecting continued until—

—Mining? What for?

—For minerals essential to the manipulation of microwave frequencies. The Grand Iyama held up a milky quartz from its fruit-bowl. —On the Rose we are limited, you see.

All Sinclair saw was Sherlock Holmes holding up a very ordinary stone between finger and thumb and smiling.

—What's your point? he asked carefully.

—That our doorways be closed. That miners withdraw. That cruelties cease on both sides. That Iyama be given back.

—What do you mean, given back?

—Many are kept in secret installations. Our agents are everywhere.

The Snow Queen nodded down at him from the heights of her glittering throne. Sinclair felt funny then. It was hard to listen to the words and not be distracted by the constantly-changing face.

—What can I do about that? he said. What am I, King of the World?

—You're different, Darth Vader said.

—So I'm different, so what can I do?

185

—Tell me why they kill us, the Big Green said as the twelfth Dalai Lama, the wounds of the world in his face.

—You shouldn't have sunk the *Dayton Ohio*, Sinclair Kuet accused.

The Iyama shook his Tibetan head. —Your arrival sunk it, *Jalignah*. A new doorway – the Awfulness of your Coming—

So. In flashing from the China House he'd done more than turn into a fish. Sinclair swallowed. Aunt Ping had made the second flash which had woken poor Alma in her boat, a lonely survivor on a sullen sea which he'd risen from to join her . . .

Tell me why they kill us.

—I don't know, Sinclair said, hopelessly. —But you kill us as well. I'm not who you think I am. I come from the Chinese takeaway on the High St in Wortham and my parents don't know where I've gone and my mum might cry, which means she's sad. And where I come from, right, it's *like* this world but it *isn't* like it—

—There are many doors to my father's house.

—That's what Mr Davey said.

—And many more things you should know.

One thing he burned to know. Sinclair felt he would burst.

—Your agents – do they come – I mean, where *I* come from, would they come there?

—Enough! Napes rose.

—Wait. The Dalai Lama held up his arm. —We

can't tell what may make a difference. In answer to your question, *our agents are everywhere.*

—I want my Aunt Ping back, Sinclair said. —And I want to go home *now.*

—It is as it should be. *Jalignah* speaks.

The Dalai Lama smiled.

—I just flashed on the weirdest thing, Sinclair told Alma, ducking along in the crowd. —They think I'm here to save them.

—Who?

—The Iyama. They think I'm called Jellybum or something, and what I do makes a diff—

What he did next made a difference.

—Wait for me! Redmond screamed. Sinclair saw at a glance that Redmond was not seriously injured. Ripping a strip of braid from his dung-soiled bus monkey's uniform, he bound up poor Redmond's arm the best way he could.

—Try that, Kev, he whispered.

—Kevin/Redmond nodded. —Cheers, mate, he said.

—We must go—

Alma was right. Lions Square was no longer safe as the Maser-bolts picked out the Lions Life Building in electric bursts of radiation. But Sinclair couldn't stand to go while the war of the worlds raged on. It was like every B-movie he'd ever seen. The world destroyed by horrible aliens that killed people for no good reason. Except there *was* a reason.

—I don't believe this, he said.—I can't just—

—Sinclair! Come *on!*

—Wait!

Mounting Blamey's soap box, Sinclair raised his arms.

—I don't believe this is happening! he said. This is what happens in *films*.

The giant screen behind him flashed news from around the world. A mudslide raced through a mountain village; children cried in the road; somewhere a cat had got caught in a pipe. Some of it, or all of it, mattered.

—*Listen*, will you? Sinclair glowered down, and something in his eye caught the crowd. —This needn't happen, Sinclair told the sea of heads sternly. —It's all your own fault, you know. You need to stop now and *talk*. They *want* to talk, you'll see—

—You're one of *them*, someone cried.

—No, I'm one of *us*, Sinclair insisted. —They don't want to hurt us. It's just that they're confused. They don't understand why we trap them and farm them. I'm different. I understand.

—*What can we do?* The crowd heaved in its desire for him to tell them. —*Tell us, what can we do?*

—You should speak to the Grand Iyama—

—*But how?* the crowd heaved. —*Tell us how . . .*

A Maser-bolt lit up the screen above him. The Grand Iyama appeared as President Coleridge.

—**This is your leader**, it said. —**Please return all Iyama held in military installations. Please** release all those on farms—

Someone screamed as the Big Green changed faces from President Coleridge to Ginger Rich, fifteen-year-old Head of the Senate.

—**Please close all doorways. Please decommission the *Dayton Ohio* and all similar spy vessels**—

—*The president's Iyama!* It ran through the crowd like an electric current. *The President's one of them – President Coleridge is Iyama*—

—WAIT – YOU'VE GOT IT WRONG! Sinclair held up his hands. HE'S LOOKING LIKE THAT TO MAKE YOU *LISTEN* – DON'T YOU UNDERSTAND?

They didn't understand at all.

—Well done, you've made it worse.

Alma was right. They would never understand.

—Judgement Day is upon us! Abel Blamey raved, as the screen dimmed and the crowd turned with a roar to clear the Square, darkening by the minute under crackling electricity-laden clouds.

—*They're bringing the Magnetron in!* Sinclair considered his band. It included Alma Brand, Abel Blamey, Mae Ling Peters, Big Wolfie C, Kevin/ Redmond Lee and the entire company of the *Dayton Ohio*, Captain Bonaventure, the boy Everard and Alma's mother included, who had found each other in the crowd, and a large goat with a carrier bag caught on its horns, which seemed to have attached itself to them. He was responsible; what could he do to save them? *Help me,* he thought. *I want to go home. Robert Ames, where are you?*

Above them the rings of the Magnetron hummed with enormous bursts of amplified radiation that would ignite a building from fifty yards and burst a cow like an egg in a microwave. In effect, they were in a microwave. A mike as big as a city.

—*Run!* Alma screamed. And they ran.

And as they ran, Sinclair thought. And as he thought it occurred to him that nothing would save them now but thinking things out. *Minerals essential to the manipulation of microwave frequencies . . .* that was what the Big Green had said. He knew that anyway. *Masers make use of those transitions in crystals that correspond to the energies of microwave frequencies, Microsoft Encarta, 1998.* A cool breeze of reason blew down on him. That was Robert Ames' present.

—Under the Magnetron! Sinclair screamed.

—Are you kidding?

—*Get right under it!*

Sinclair grabbed stones as he ran; any kind, any way he could get them. Lucky for them they weren't far from the Park – the quartz in the walls would do nicely – and what were these? Crystals from some New Age stall, up-ended in the middle of the road?

Sinclair skated on jades.

—Kev – help me get these stones—

Terrific magnetic fields made Kevin Lee stagger; but he didn't ask why; he just did it.

Hardly able to stand himself, Sinclair laid out his collection.

—We should . . . protect ourselves with . . . metal, Boney opined belatedly.

Probably Captain Bonaventure was right. But these 'waves would fry you anyway. A circle of stones surrounded them now. It was the best he could do. Different crystals, different frequencies . . . he hoped. They seemed pretty puny . . . but still . . .

—Keep inside the crystals! Sinclair warned his band, as they grouped around a statue of a monkey. There was nowhere else to run to. It was as good a place as any to meet the end of the world.

The giant Magnetron descended above them, the flow of ions in its vacuum tubes pitching enough magnetism to bend the shape of the earth and create enough amplified radiation to recharge a million Masers. The battle seemed distant now. His hair stood on end and the bones in Sinclair's body hummed to the tune of the rings above, a tune that would cook them at any minute and turn them out like a fricassee.

—*We're going to die, aren't we?* Kevin Lee's eyes appealed to him. Alma hugged her mother; Abel Blamey raved quietly to himself; Mae Ling held him tightly.

It was as if some giant hand were poised over a microwave button. Sinclair felt his teeth chatter together. Enormous pressures built up in his chest.

Something was about to happen.

19

THE KEVIN LEE REVERSAL

Bing!

—Seems all right to me, Sinclair's dad said, testing the microwave. —Heaven knows what caused this mess.

He picked up a pair of blackened trainers, placed precisely in front of the microwave, and smelled them in a puzzled way. Size 10's. Pretty burnt. Whose trainers were they?

—Ping should know. He scratched his head. —But where is she?

—You shouldn't run that microwave while it's empty, Sinclair's mother said, with only a hazy idea how it worked. —It makes the microwaves bang together.

—I know that, I've just cleaned it out, Sinclair's father snapped. —How about this mess on the walls? What's all that about?

—I don't know, but most of it's off. Sinclair's mother wiped her Jif-stained hands on her apron. —I'm exhausted now. You have *a single night off* and it's chaos—

—Can I have number eighty-three please, and two egg-fried rice and a spring roll? David Selwyn asked pleasantly, in later than usual that night. —Did you have a fire in here, or something?

—Just testing. Sinclair's dad took the order and tried to laugh it off. Out of the side of his mouth he said, —*It's got something to do with Sinclair, take it from me.*

He popped a dish of pre-cooked rice into the microwave by the strip-curtain.

—Won't be a minute, he said. —Let me try this again.

His finger hovered and jabbed the button – Cook – OK – *2 mins.*

The dish began to rotate and the magnetron to generate microwaves that were, unbeknownst to Daddy Kuet, almost as dangerous as ever, but lucky for him, slightly weakened.

—Taking its time, isn't it? he said. He looked around at his customers. All of them had come in in the last ten minutes, drawn as if by a magnet as the shop had come to life. Since they'd walked in and found the shop empty, re-kindled the heat under the woks and tried to clear up the mess, at least six orders had come in. *If you wanted something done properly*, Daddy Kuet supposed, *you had to do it yourself.* All the same, it wasn't like Ping. He supposed there'd been a fire and she'd gone for help. The takings were still in the till. Why would she go out and leave it? Where was everybody? How long had that dog been tied to that

193

chair? Was anyone coming to claim it? Probably Sinclair would know. It occurred to him that Sinclair must be somewhere.

—Anyone seen a boy, about ten, with glasses and a yellow jumper? fat Daddy Kuet asked all four walls of his takeaway.

In the moment Sinclair's father's finger descended on the 'cook' button on the mike in the takeaway kitchen, the massed Maser-bolts of the Greenback army converged on the head of the monkey-statue in Animal City and blew Sinclair's band clean away through some mysterious doorway. Sinclair had had plenty of time to think about it as he tumbled through time and space.

Hadn't he fulfilled his promise to save them all – all except Wolfie? Was it *his* fault that only those who had come through a doorway one way, could go back the same way again? All the same, he wished he'd known what might happen. Poor Wolfie's face had been burned on his memory forever in the moment of leaving.

—*Don't leave me behind!* Wolfie had cried, pathetically. —*I'm thirteen next week – they'll kill me!*

His arms had waved in the air; he threw back his head, searching upwards; his mouth had opened and closed.

—*Edgecumbe! Wait for me!*

Sinclair looked down through a tunnel of light. He had an impression his face was looking down from the sky, and that Wolfie could see it. Through a tunnel of light, with an enormous arm made of light, he reached down and plucked up Parky out of the crowd.

—DON'T WORRY, he said in an enormous voice, as the tunnel narrowed and Wolfie's pleading face grew more and more distant. —DON'T WORRY, WE'VE GOT PARKY, AND HATHURST'S IYAMA, ANYWAY. BIG WOLFIE C, *FREE THE RANK . . . THAT'S WHAT YOU'VE GOT TO DO . . .*

He thought he saw Alma wave to him. —*Sinclair! Sinclair, goodbye!*

—*I think we should take the Police Chief,* he thought he told Mae Ling, perhaps because he looked familiar, somehow, on his dashing black horse way below them.

—*Leave him,* Mae Ling seemed to say. —*He only looks like Mr Niles.*

Wolfie's face had been swallowed up and so had the war over Animal City and the multitude below him. He remembered not a lot after that. Darkness rushing by; a million flashing suns; a misty place filled with pilots. It was, Mae Ling thought, as she tumbled with Kevin Lee, a *Kevin Lee Reversal* situation. Where in the world would she land next? Who would she be, when she got there? This was what had happened before. *Only now, it was happening more slowly.*

Sinclair noticed the difference. It was a subtly different frequency to the one that had rearranged his molecules before, when he'd carelessly microwaved Daisy. But at least it was one that hadn't killed them.

The crystals he'd placed so carefully, however small, had caused the magnetic field generated by the Magnetron to vary. By varying the magnetic field he'd found a different microwave frequency, usefully one that hadn't fried them. That was the theory at least, Sinclair thought, whilst upside down in some strange space he didn't like to think about too much . . .

It seemed to Sinclair then that he sat once more in a boat in the phosphorescent night of his dream. While he was thinking about it, the Lady in Colours dropped by. She had a kindly pale face and stroked him very gently on his neck with her trailing scarves. Beneath him, Fish World glimmered. The Lady in Colours approached over the water and breathed on his neck very gently.

He looked up into her changing face. —*Who are you*, he breathed. —*Do I know you?*

—*You know me very well*. The Lady in Colours smiled.—*I live in a tank in the shop. I jumped out, once – remember?*

Sinclair flinched.—*You're Daisy?*

Daisy showed her colours.—*I didn't like going round.*

—*Going round?*

—*In the microwave. It hurt.*

—*Oh*. Sinclair felt that he hurt all over. —*Oh. Of course it did.*

The Lady in Colours touched him; he looked; and his lateral lines were gone.

—*You're no more a fish than I am.*

—*No . . . of course I'm not . . .*

196

The Lady in Colours drew her scarves over his face, and Sinclair slept again. This time it seemed to him he was floating in a powder-blue universe. In the distance floated a rose the size of a planet. A long string of objects encircled it – a traffic cone, a wardrobe, a dentist; a wheelbarrow, a ship, a bus; a chimney, a cat, very like Dim Sum; a table, a chair, a—

—*Aunt Ping!*

Aunt Ping joined him and smiled. —*Sinclair!* she said. —*What a long time!* And yet it had been only moments, whatever moments were.

—*Take a good look*, she said.—*Not everyone glimpses the Rose.*

Sinclair looked back at the Rose Planet and glimpsed it from every angle before Aunt Ping took his arm.

—*Beautiful, isn't it?* she seemed to say. —*The most beautiful thing in the world.*

He thought he saw Iyama.

—*Is that where they come from?* he said.

Aunt Ping nodded mysteriously.

—*They come from the heart of the flower.*

The heart of the flower. The strange phrase seemed to grip him and mingle with the smell of noodles. A long tunnel opened before him; Sinclair saw Kevin Lee's feet and legs somersaulting past him as they fell. He had the strangest feeling he was being lengthened or squeezed, as though in some pasta machine. Just as he felt he couldn't be lengthened any more, and that his blood would squirt out of his feet and he'd loop down on to someone's plate like some kind of human spaghetti, the squeezing stopped and a million lights flashed and Sinclair plopped sprawling, along with everyone else, onto the hessian-matted floor of the China House Takeaway on Wortham High St at almost exactly twenty-past nine of a sultry and quite busy evening.

Bing!

—Oh! Sinclair got up. The smell of noodles overwhelmed him. He felt himself all over. Kevin Lee got up beside him; then Mae Ling; then Monahan. Aunt Ping looked around. —Where's Dim Sum?

Last to get up was Mr Davey. He wasn't entirely himself.

—*Whaa–?* Neither was David Selwyn. —*Whaa?* he said, again, at the sight of a sudden dump of people he knew in the middle of the takeaway, out of nowhere.

—*Wha? Where?* He didn't get much further.

Several other customers backed away.

—Did you *see* that?

—Where did they *come* from?

—They must have come in at the door—

—They didn't, though, did they?

—They *must* have—

—Sinclair! There you are! His mother emerged from the kitchen. —I want a word with you, young man!

His mother was funny, Sinclair decided. Didn't she *see* what he looked like? So busy that her eyes ran over him as though he might normally turn up in a strange, ripped uniform with a bunch of other singed people, Mrs Kuet ran on:

—Has anyone seen any bags? I'm out of boxes completely, and I don't know what I'm going to put an order for six in—

Sinclair looked around him. The puzzlingly-burned walls of the takeaway had never looked so sweet, the smell of frying noodles never so intoxicatingly wonderful. It was the smell of *home*.

—*Mum!* Sinclair hugged his mother as he'd never hugged her before. He felt quite different, really. Like he knew what hugging was about.

—Sinclair, you have some explaining to do. Mrs Kuet detached him.

—Mrs Kuet, they just appeared from *nowhere!* David Selwyn recovered his mouth, hanging open so long that a thin trail of dribble had escaped.

—This had better be good, Sinclair. Sinclair's mother searched his face. —I want to know where you've *been. And* why the kitchen was burned. Ping, you might say something.

Ping tried, but no words came.

—Well? Sinclair's mother waited.

—W-where I've *been?* Sinclair stammered. A million scenes flashed across his mind. Fish World, gleaming under the water; the junk *Annaho*, plying the southern seas with her russet sails bent under the wind; the hold; the flash of Masers; Animal City by night in all its jewels; Robert Ames' half-weary face; the rank, with its spangled bus monkeys; the thin white hand of the Iyama-man under the bus; the killing ramp at the farm; the blood-red sky over the battle; the Grand Iyama with his hundred faces; the Lady in Colours, smiling across the water; the wonderful world of the Rose . . .

—*I've* been somewhere, me. Kevin Lee scratched his head. —I don't know *where* I've been, but I hurt my arm while I was there—

And Kevin-that-had-been-Redmond displayed his badly-cut elbow.

Mae Ling had memories of her own. The Sweeper, sweeping for life-forms; the grass votives sprinkled off the Sheep Tower, blowing away on the wind over the Animal City; Iyama-corpses turning in the warehouse; the whistles, bangs and sirens of the City; Pitt the Younger, flourishing his spoon; her ride on Adamantine.

I don't know where I've been . . .

Where *have* we been? she wondered.

20

FEELING FOR DAISY

—I don't know what came over me. Mr Davey rubbed his head. —I thought I was some kind of *preacher*.

—Abel Blamey. Sinclair grinned. —I *told* you I knew who you were.

—'The end of the world is nigh', Mae Ling teased him.

Mr Davey shook his head.

—It almost *was*, Sinclair said.

The survivors of inter-dimensional travel and wars with hostile aliens shared a cocoa in the flat upstairs. Beneath them the takeaway was winding down business for the night. Explanations for the evening's weird happenings had come and gone as quickly as bean-sprouts into a wok; but the final word had been Monahan's.

—I left the wok on, Aunt Ping wailed.

—I turned it off, said Monahan.

—Did I miss something here? David Selwyn looked from one to the other.

—Everything, Mae Ling told him.

—But Napes—? Sinclair wondered.

—He only *looked* like David, Mae Ling insisted. —It's bound to happen in parallel worlds. Just like I looked like Jessica, whoever she was.

Poor David Selwyn's head twitched from side to side like a spectator at a tennis tournament; so did Daddy Kuet's, and he still wasn't any the wiser.

—So let me get this straight. Sinclair's father tried to make sense of it. —The microwave *banged* you somewhere—

Sinclair nodded enthusiastically. These were his very words.

—and you visited Veggie World, where people eat aliens that look—

—that *can* look—

—that *can* look like people, but they snap into dinosaur-things – and there's a war on. And while you were gone, the wok set fire to the kitchen—

—And *I* put it out. Monahan drew himself up. —You owe me your business, Kuet.

—You're not going to back up this stupid story? Daddy Kuet searched Monahan's face.

—As far as that goes – Monahan paused. A succession of emotions more complex than he was used to dealing with seemed to chase one another across his hammer-headed face – as far as that goes, I *did* put something in the microwave. I must have nodded off. I dreamt I worked on a bus rank, and I kidnapped boys to run it.

—If you say so, Mr Monahan. Daddy Kuet raised his eyebrows.

—I *do* say so. Monahan stuck out his face—
Something funny happened here, Kuet. He held up
his blackened trainers—But if a *word* of this reaches
outside these four walls, there's no telling where it'll
get to. It didn't happen, right?

Monahan turned to glare at them all, and in his
Parky voice barked:

—We had a little chip-fire, right? And otherwise an
ordinary evening?

—Otherwise an ordinary evening, everyone had
droned.

Mollified, Monahan had left them.

That had been two hours ago now. Now Monahan
slept like a baby in his horrible chrome-filled flat.
Completely right all the time, by morning he would
have convinced himself that nothing had happened.
He'd put out a little kitchen fire, then fallen asleep
and dreamed some strange dreams in the process. That
was all there was to it. He wasn't the airy-fairy type.

Eleven twenty-four, said the clock on the kitchen
wall. Sinclair's father and mother would work on 'til
midnight in the shop below to catch the late crop of
customers turning out of the pubs.

The kitchen window stood open on a thunder-
warm night. Beneath it the neon sign hummed:

CHINA HOUSE TAKEAWAY
Quality Chinese Food

—What about Mr Niles, Mae Ling said. —Did

he ever get his chicken curry?

—I think he went out to move his car, someone said.

She'd been about to serve him, she remembered, in the moments before she'd been 'banged away', as Sinclair would describe it. The face of Police Chief Cherry rose in front of her.

Adamantine, the thought whispered, deep in her mind. *Please let the war not kill him.*

In fact it had ended as suddenly as it had started. The-War-That-Never-Was went down in Iyama legend something like this:

'*And* Jalignah *came. Put up your Masers, he said.* Jalignah *speaks. I want my Aar-Ping now. And Aar-Ping meant the End-of-all-Wars; and* Jalignah *ascended in the Light of the Last of Battles. And the doorway was closed forever and the day of the Primrose was done.*'

Wolfie had woken up one morning and posted a message. He didn't know why, or if it would get there, or even why he felt he had to *do* it; but he did it anyway, and something had told him it would work: EDGECUMBE THE WAR IS OVER*EVERYTHING IS COOL*YOURS THE FREE RANK OF BUSLINK*EDGECUMBE THE WAR IS OVER*EVERYTHING IS COOL*YOURS THE FREE RANK OF BUSLINK*EDGECUMBE THE WAR IS OVER*EVERYTHING IS COOL*YOU

It had cost a mint to hire the electronic screen in Lions Square to broadcast his message over the animals, people and not-so-hidden Iyama of the Animal City, but Wolfie knew it was worth it. The Co-operative CityBus Company of the Free Rank could stand a little advertising, in any case. They'd all agreed on that. The message had come to him that morning. Somehow, Wolfie felt sure, it would leak across; somewhere, wherever he'd gone to, Edgecumbe would read it and be glad that the world – that *this* world – hadn't ended.

It had its problems, of course. But since The-War-That-Never-Was, Iyama farms everywhere had folded by law, and Iyama-meat was as big a no-no as pig-meat, cow-meat, or *any* kind of meat in Veggie World. A new law had been drafted; the constitution amended; it was held as self-evident now that aliens be accorded respect, the same as any mollusc. Animal City slept sounder at night. No one checked for Iyama any more; Iyama were a fact of life. One day they would apply for jobs; have rights under City law. The lessons of the war that *almost* was would not be forgotten by its citizens. Intolerance would no longer be tolerated. Wolfie smiled when he thought of it. He wanted every world there *was* to know, Edgecumbe's most of all.

Sinclair had been watching 'ER' when the message had flashed onscreen.

USLINK*EDGECUMBE THE WAR IS OVER* EVERYTHING IS COOL*YOURS THE FREE

—Did you see that? Sinclair blinked.

THE FREE RANK OF BUSLINK*EDGECUMBE
THE WAR IS OVER*EVERYTHING IS COOL

—What?

IS COOL*YOURS THE FREE RANK OF
BUSLINK*EDGECUMBE THE WAR IS OVER

—That message?
—What message?
—That message that just came onscreen.

Sinclair's mother had shrugged. —You're seeing
things, she told him.

But Mae Ling's eyes were bright. She threw Sinclair
a look that set him tingling from head to foot. *She'd*
seen the message, all right. Adamantine rode on in her
dreams, undisturbed by Masers, his perfect black feet
flashing, his single-minded patrol of the streets
undimmed by any war.

Sinclair was happy after that, in that best of all
possible worlds, his own.

He raised his game at school.

—Sinclair's a lot more *sociable* these days, Mr Davey
swore at Parents Evening. —His relationship skills are
improving by leaps and bounds, they really are, Mrs
Kuet.

His art teacher, Mrs Rayburn, agreed:

—His drawings are much more *personal* now.
Especially the ones of Pig City.

—Pig City?

Sinclair's mother looked puzzled. Mrs Rayburn showed her.

The drawings spilled out of a roll on the desk; at least twenty showed 'Pig City' in incredible detail, down to the fluting on the Sheep Tower. The big difference was, there were people; not only people, but animals – even the odd Iyama.

—It's the first time I've seen him draw people.

Sinclair's mother had a lump in her throat. Her funny son had a heart, of course. Every day he showed her more of it.

Sinclair watched his teacher examine his drawings. They didn't seem exceptional to him. They were simply echoes of the Animal City. Its echoes were all around him.

—I love this one of the city by night, Mrs Rayburn enthused. —I saw what Sinclair was trying to do, so we tried it with chalk on black paper – look at this central figure, so *sympathetic* – and the lights of the city behind him, you see, make a sort of crown for his head—

—It's amazing, Sinclair's mother agreed. She pointed to the tall central figure, its arms upraised like a saint.

—Someone you know? she asked Sinclair.

Sinclair nodded carefully. He wasn't about to tell her who.

—They show a *personal perspective*, you see, something quite new for Sinclair. Mrs Rayburn couldn't say enough. —And a feeling for animals that's extraordinary—

—What's that? Mrs Kuet pointed again.

Mrs Rayburn turned to Sinclair, her finger on an Iyama peering around the corner of a building. — What's this, Sinclair — a monster?

—It's an alien. I don't do monsters.

—A friendly alien? His mother joked.

Sinclair raised his eyebrows.

—What other kind are there? he said.

Sinclair enjoyed their attention. His mother was pleased with him. His teachers were pleased with him. For a first, he was pleased with himself. As well as calculating orders, he now had a key to people. Instead of being puzzled by the noises and faces they made, since his feelings for dumb Iyama, he now had a clue how it felt to be misunderstood. He also had feelings for Daisy.

Ever after that, he changed the water in her tank every week.

—You don't need to do that, Cousin Sang told him.

—Yuh-huh. I think I *do*.

—There's plenty of oxygen in the water. That's what the aerator's for.

Tiring of argument, Sinclair would put his hands on his hips and knock down any objection.

—You don't know, he'd begin. —How d'you think it *feels* to be a fish in a tank? For a start, you need fresh water. Else you feel like you've got a headache.

Fish don't get headaches, someone would tell him. Then Sinclair would say, —I should *know*; and he'd finish refreshing Daisy's tank and tenderly replace her.

And Daisy would fan out her tropical fins and repay him with a show of all her colours. Soon Sinclair got more Daisies; soon he had a whole tank; ten were enough, he'd explain. Any more, and war would break out.

His family got used to his tropical fish obsession in the end, and Sinclair got used to them being used to it. He knew that obsessing over tropical fish made him a bit of an anorak, but he wasn't about to let that stop him. He might have a shop one day, and sell fish to make a living. He knew all about them – he'd *been* one – how more expert could he be? He would never be the same as everyone else. Different was good, wasn't it?

So Sinclair went on day by day, doing the best that he could and feeling for anything helpless, most especially because most creatures couldn't speak up to tell you how they were feeling for themselves. Mae Ling approved so thoroughly, she thought she'd never known Sinclair. This was a Sinclair everyone loved; a Sinclair who would sooner put his own toe through the rusty old mangle in the shed, than the tadpoles he used to put through it when he was six; a Sinclair who had volunteered for 'Toadwatch' and had gone out all night with a fluorescent jacket and a bucket to help mating toads cross an A-road, because that's what he needed to do; a feeling Sinclair, a Sinclair she sensed crossed the world between humans and animals more easily than she ever could.

But he hadn't *quite* closed the gap between worlds.

Even when the battered old microwave sat waiting in the back of the car for his father to take it to the dump, and a shining new microwave sat waiting in its place in the kitchen, Sinclair had echoes in his mind.

Little things reminded him.

One day, on the school bus, he thought he glimpsed a shop called *Clones*. Next day, he looked again, but it wasn't there. Every day after that he searched for the shop, as the bus passed endless similar parades of shops, but he never saw it again. Yet he was sure that he'd seen it. *Clones*. Like the little, twisted shop-front where he'd bought simulated chicken-parts as a bus-boy, for all the eagle hawks that had nodded to work on his Topper in New Pork.

Other things reminded him.

One time, on a trip to town, he thought he heard a war-cry:

EEE-YOAR-*OH!* EEE-YOAR-*OH-A!*

Then he realised it was the paper-man, who always called on the corner:

—YOUR – EVE'NIN-HER-*AL!* EVE'NIN-HER-*AL!*

The *Evening Herald*, he meant. Why couldn't he call it more clearly? One thing that was clear, was that the things which seemed to hold echoes for Sinclair soon melted away into ordinary things, the more he looked into them. The wall between worlds was complete, probably a good thing, since things shouldn't 'leak' between them. Probably the shop he'd seen had been called *Bones* or *Jones* or *Phones* or something.

Probably he didn't even see it.

Sinclair had just about convinced himself. Then one evening something happened to overturn his world so thoroughly that Sinclair was back to square one, or square minus a million, or whatever came before it.

It happened the night his parents had gone to see friends. Aunt Ping's night 'on' usually meant more help from Sinclair. Already he'd taken ten orders, and it wasn't even half-past seven. The rush lasted 'til half-past eight. Then a Tuesday-night lull set in, and Sinclair half-dozed at his counter.

He hardly heard the door ding; hardly looked up when a long shadow fell over his menu.

—Can I take your order? he said, automatically turning a new leaf on his order pad. He didn't even bother looking up until the pause before someone should say something went on a moment too long. But when he did, he forgot about anything else that had ever existed.

—*Oh!* Sinclair balked.

—Can you take my order? Robert Ames showed his teeth in a brilliant smile. —Let's see – squid, if you have it; otherwise, a fine mess of noodles. What else can you recommend?

Sinclair felt quite frightened.

—I don't know, I—

—Don't you know me, shipmate? There's many another would like to catch up with me, I can tell you.

Sinclair felt his heart would burst. *Robert Ames, Robert Ames, Robert Ames*—

211

—It's hard, Robert Ames complained, —when one shipmate don't know another, though they bunk down together under the stars *ever* so many nights—

—*But they burned you!* Sinclair burst out, suddenly back on the docks that night, tears coursing down his face.

The Teller of Tales threw back his head and laughed.

—Oho, wouldn't they like to! No, shipmate – He brought his intense brown eyes to bear – I didn't burn. *I dived.*

—You dived? Sinclair repeated stupidly.

—Like a seal. The brown eyes burned. —In at the deep end of the dock, I can tell you; but old Bob Ames, he knows when to keep his head down.

He didn't look old. With his sun-browned limbs under his sailcloth shirt itching for any kind of action, his eyes brimming with sauce, and his tongue with tales of derring-do, he didn't look old at all. He looked, in fact, like a sun-browned boy who plays in the sand all day, and doesn't know when to stop.

Sinclair warmed under the unexpected sun of Robert Ames' lost smile.

—I'm *so* glad they didn't kill you, he whispered. —I wish I'd known before.

Robert Ames tapped his nose.

—Play it close to your chest, he said. —You won't go blowing any whistles on poor Bob Ames?

—Of course not. Sinclair felt faint. As if he'd betray Robert Ames. —But what are you doing here?

—Secret orders. Ames winked. —But I've got to

keep my sails trimmed see, and tack a bit tight to the wind.

Secret orders. Something about the phrase chilled Sinclair to the bone. He wished Robert Ames hadn't used it. *Our agents are everywhere.* Where had *that* phrase come from?

—Sinclair, is that an order? Aunt Ping shouted from the kitchen.

—Not yet, no, Sinclair called back quickly, his own voice sounding strange to him against the hiss of the fryers. He'd forgotten his aunt was there, or that orders were what he was supposed to be taking.

—Look sharp! I'd better be gone! Robert Ames looked hunted.

—Can you peel me some mushrooms, then? Aunt Ping called through the strip-curtain.

Sinclair wished she'd shut up.

—Please, he said. —Don't go—

Slipping a note to Sinclair, Robert Ames turned at the door. —Wrote that in case I missed you. I've missed you before, like a fool.

—You've been *before?*

—Had my eye on you, shipmate. —Robert Ames saluted. —A.1. to see you so lively.

—Wait – don't go yet – please!

Sinclair threw himself round his counter; but the door had almost closed itself as silently as Bob Ames had opened it, by the time he got out onto the street. Something gleamed on the pavement. Sinclair picked it up.

—Wait! he shouted – *You dropped something!*

But the running figure didn't stop. It bobbed at the end of the High Street; and dipped away right in Bread Lane. There was no point in running after it. It would out-pace a greyhound to see it go, and Sinclair wasn't the fastest.

He trailed back inside the China House like someone who'd just found Christmas and lost it again. It wasn't until he'd returned to his post at the counter, that his eye fell on Bob Ames' note:

My Lad—

Meet me at midnight, the night of the fourth, by the Inn called The Bell Jar in town; keep it under your hat until then that you've clapped eyes on

R.L. Ames.

Something a bit funny about it. Robert Ames had never, to Sinclair's knowledge, called him 'my lad'. It sounded like something someone would write, who thought they knew Robert Ames. Sinclair folded the note. He couldn't quite believe it, but the wall between worlds had come down. A new doorway must have opened somewhere, a doorway from that world, to this; he'd never dreamed, for some reason, it could work the other way round; and where Robert Ames had led the way, others could follow. *Was that such a good thing*, a chill down his back made him wonder – but how could he doubt it? Any wind that blew him Robert Ames' smile, was a wind set fair for Sinclair.

But still . . .

What had he asked the Big Green? Where *I* come

from, would they come there? *Our agents are everywhere.* That phrase. It came from the conversation with the Grand Iyama. The Grand Iyama had said there were spies. Spies could come through the wall.

It was then that Sinclair opened his hand. The thing Robert Ames had dropped as he brushed past the door was small and hard, like a toenail – small and perfect and loaded with meaning, it lay in his palm though he wished he'd missed it, and meant that everything in every world had changed.

The thing Robert Ames had dropped.

The thing he – Sinclair – had picked up to hand him back.

As if he were human, after all.

And worth handing something back to.

As if he hadn't been lying forever.

As if the thing in Sinclair's hand wasn't

a single, blue-red spine.

QUIRX 1: WELCOME TO INNER SPACE

Lesley Howarth

A world just on the edge . . .

An off-beat world bursting to climb out of its cage, just a blink away from everyday reality.

A world where the fantastic and the bizarre, the strange and the uncanny, are just a heartbreat away.

QUIRX. Beyond words.

Ever been bugged by a feverish dream? Or been so scared by a video you watch it through shreddies. Wondered why school bus drivers are such grouches? Or let eavesdropping get you into *terrible* trouble?

Welcome to Inner Space.
Nothing will ever be the same again.